Laurel Cove

To: Lauri,
 Thank you so much
 for reading my story!
 Sarah Taborna

Laurel Cove

Sarah Turtle

SAPPHIRE BOOKS

SALINAS, CALIFORNIA

ISBN - 978-1-948232-53-1

Editor - Kaycee Hawn
Book Design - LJ Reynolds
Cover Design - Fineline Cover Design

Sapphire Books Publishing, LLC
P.O. Box 8142
Salinas, CA 93912
www.sapphirebooks.com

Printed in the United States of America
First Edition – March 2019

This and other Sapphire Books titles can be found at
www.sapphirebooks.com

Dedication

For Kamalei.

Acknowledgments

The single most important element to the writing process for myself is time. I can have stories in my head, but if I don't have time to get them out on paper, then my creativity is trapped in the confines of my mind. Kamalei has graciously offered for me to have all the time I need to bring my stories to life on the pages of books and for this I will be eternally grateful. I was fortunate to have a whimsical childhood in which my parents encouraged me to explore my imaginative side. They supported my love of books with weekly trips to the bookstore. They provided me with a collection of stories that filled shelves as well as my mind with ideas, which in turn shaped the future of my love of writing. I will be forever thankful that they have always supported my decision to become a writer.

Lastly, every aspiring author needs just one publishing company to take a chance on them. I thank Christine at Sapphire Books for this opportunity to publish my debut novel, and to Kaycee for making the editing process an easy one.

Chapter One

illa slid off her glasses and rubbed at her eyes before replacing them and typing rapidly at the keyboard on her laptop. In the time it took her to read over the new lines she just wrote, she quickly swept her flowing blond hair up into a messy pile at the top of her head. It didn't look pretty, but at this hour of the night, no one was left in their offices to notice.

Those employed at the publishing company teased Willa at how odd it was for her to have requested an office space in the building, when all the other authors prided themselves on having the ability to work from anywhere they pleased. Willa decided early on in her writing career that she needed the structure of going to a workplace if she intended to get anything done with the least amount of procrastination possible. Her publisher most certainly did not complain because Willa paid rent for the space and was always early for hitting deadlines.

A buzzing sound, followed by a chime, went off on the cell phone that Willa tore her eyes away from the computer screen to glance at. She scowled at the unknown number flashing and pushed the button to send it to voicemail. Her dark eyes fell once again into a deep state of concentration as she focused on completing the chapter she was writing.

Less than a minute passed when the cell phone once again lit up with the same unknown number. Willa growled in frustration at the distraction and resorted to shutting the phone down completely to avoid dealing with it going off during her most productive writing session of the week. This time, though, her mind continually shifted back from her story to the reason why two calls in a row without a voicemail were necessary. It took twice as long as it should have for her to type the next sentence due to the worry that started to settle in the back of Willa's mind.

A shrill sound that made Willa jerk up in her seat, rang from the corner of her desk. The office phone that had been installed but never used was now going off for the first time in all the years she had been there. Not being an actual working employee of the publishing company made it so that the phone was really quite useless, but the building required it for emergency purposes. Willa peered out at the multiple empty desks that were visible from her office space and then back at the phone as if it was a forbidden act to answer it.

She picked up the receiver from the charging cradle and fumbled her fingers over the buttons. Willa couldn't even remember the last time she had used a landline phone and the keypad was like a foreign object in her hand. She pushed the green talk button and raised it to her ear. "Hello?"

The caller on the other line hesitated for a moment and then responded. "Am I speaking to Willa Barton?"

Willa sighed heavily, already annoyed that somehow a call had made its way to her office. She craned her neck to try and see if anyone out in the reception area could have possibly transferred the call into her by accident. Knowing full well she was alone other than the occasional cleaning person or security officer that passed by, she groaned and answered. "This is Willa, but I'm not sure how you got through to this extension. You need to speak to my agent for booking interviews or events. I'll send you through to her voicemail." Willa reached over to the phone base and frantically tried to figure out how to get rid of the caller as soon as possible.

Before she could decipher the phone system, the voice of the elderly woman stopped Willa's actions with just a few simple words. "Willa, this is your Aunt Beth."

It would have been an inconvenience to have to deal with talking to a member of the press or someone else looking to interview her, and even more annoying to talk with a fan who somehow slipped through the phone system. This caller, however, was the one person that Willa always feared might contact her someday. With her mind racing with emotions, she steadied her voice and said something that wouldn't express how scared she really was. "I'm sorry; I didn't recognize your voice."

"It's understandable since you were quite young the last time we spoke."

"Yes, I was." Willa closed her eyes and rubbed a circle around her nauseated stomach. "Is everything okay?"

The lingering time it took for Beth to respond was all the answer she needed to know that this was not a simple social call between long lost relatives.

"Oh, sweetie, it's your dad…"

"What happened?" Willa hoped he was just injured or sick and she could do something to help him through his recovery.

"It was his heart; he's gone." Beth paused for a moment when her voice started to crack. "Willa, you need to come home. Come back to the Cove."

The rest of the phone call was a formality of

necessities when making arrangements after the passing of a loved one takes place. Willa didn't really pay attention to much of the conversation. All it did was leave her with a tightness in her chest as she suppressed the tears that needed to fall, but she wanted to exit the building and pass the watchful eyes of the security cameras before allowing herself to break down.

She hurriedly packed up her laptop and made her way out to the parking garage before crumpling up into the seat of her car.

It was nearly dawn by the time Willa composed herself enough to pull out onto the streets of New York towards her apartment to pack for her unexpected trip back to her childhood home, and only four hours later, she crossed the state border into Maine. Willa was aware she had been speeding most of the way, but now that the scenery had shifted from a highway to small towns as she navigated the slower paced track up Route One, she dropped down to mirror the rest of the local traffic.

After one last stop for a coffee refill, Willa stretched her arms over her head and massaged her right calf muscle to prepare for the last leg of her journey. An hour and a half later, she passed by a sign that read, 'Laurel Cove.'

The small island community was a quaint seaside village area that flooded Willa with childhood memories the instant she entered its borders. As she passed by inlets of water, rows of oak trees, and little cottages that hadn't changed a bit since the day she last drove through, a history she worked so long at forgetting came rushing back. She pushed back the images of anyone that wasn't her father. She was here for him and no one else mattered now.

Her compact sports car was clearly out of place

in a town that had a pickup truck in every driveway. She turned the air conditioning off and opened up the sunroof to inhale the salty aroma of the sea into her lungs. It was a refreshing change in comparison to the smog weighing down the air in the city.

Willa pulled into the yard of a small house. It was bittersweet to see the front porch decorated with old buoys and lobster traps. Her father was equally proud of his boat and his home so he had intertwined the themes of them together into one.

With her hand on the doorknob, Willa felt oddly both familiar and strange opening the door to the place she had lived in for eighteen years, but had not returned to since. She wasn't sure if she should knock first, knowing her aunt was inside, and yet realizing she was now the sole owner of this house. Releasing her fears in a deep breath outward, she pushed the door open, and the scents she associated with her dad and the happiest years of her life overcame her.

A pair of tall rubber boots sat just inside the entryway, which reeked of low tide mud flats, but past that, the smell of men's cologne and aftershave surrounded her like a hug from a man that would never be able to comfort her again. Just as this thought entered her mind, an embrace came from out of nowhere as her Aunt Beth squeezed her from the side.

Willa endured the awkward hug for longer than she wanted to, so as not to insult her aunt, but they had never been very close in the past and she would have preferred to be alone with her sorrow. When the tiny, gray haired woman finally released her, she shut the door, took the few steps into the center of the living room, and slumped down onto the old leather couch that felt like an old friend.

Beth settled into a wooden rocking chair across from Willa and picked up a photo album that was laying on the coffee table between them. "I was going through these and if you don't mind, I'd like to bring some to the library to have copies made for myself?"

Willa smiled to herself, pondering that the simple act of copying a photo was technology that every person had in their homes, except for the older generation, especially here on Laurel Cove, where people still lived simple lives. "Just keep the album. It's one of the older ones from before I was born. Most of the people in it I've never even met."

"Well, I suppose it won't be too long until you'll be inheriting it right back from me again."

"Aunt Beth, don't say that."

"I hope to have many years left in me, dear, but my younger brother was taken before me, and I never thought that day would come either."

"That's what years of eating nothing but steak, potatoes, and ice cream will do to you." Willa felt another surge of emotion well up inside of her as she recalled eating dinner on the fold up tables in front of the television while they watched football games together. Not wanting her aunt to see how the memory was affecting her, Willa held back the tears by covering them up with a yawn.

"You must be exhausted after such a long ride. You should go take a nap. I freshened up your bed with clean sheets."

"My bed?" Willa stood and made her way down the short hallway to a door that still had her name written on it with wooden carved letters. Upon opening the door, she gasped at the sight of a room that remained unchanged since she was eighteen years old.

Beth had come up from behind her and smiled brightly as she watched the amazement on Willa's face at the room that stood frozen in time. Willa ran her fingers over the certificates framed on the walls for writing awards and certificates for completions of advanced placement classes. She picked up a glass jar filled with movie tickets and concert stubs, then flicked the tassel on her cap from graduation that was wrapped in the valedictorian cord.

Willa turned to her aunt. "He left everything right where it was when I went away."

"Not just you, sweetie, you were too young to remember, but just about everything inside this house is just as your mother had left it after she passed."

Willa looked at Beth with a glazed over expression. She had never really thought about it before, but now she understood why her father refused to replace any of the old furniture, decorations, or even kitchen utensils with new items. It was all he had left of his wife and now he had done the same with his daughter.

Willa gripped her fingers around the edges of her dresser to steady herself. "I guess I just expected it would be different with me."

Beth rubbed the palm of her hand up and down the length of Willa's arm. "He loved you dearly, no matter what the circumstances of you leaving were."

"I should have come back here to visit him."

"Don't fret over things you didn't do. He enjoyed bragging to the men on the docks about having his daughter fly him out to the big city a few times a year." Beth dropped her hand and backed out of the room. "I'll be on my way and let you get some rest now."

"Aren't there things we should go over before you leave?"

"No, I'm in the process of making arrangements for the cremation."

"I should help you with that."

"There are so many other things that you will be busy with this week. I promise I am following the instructions according to Henry's will, as he requested."

Willa nodded. "I'm sure you are. Thank you for everything, Aunt Beth."

Beth waved a solemn goodbye as she backed out of the driveway. Willa sighed heavily, glad to be alone finally, because grieving in the presence of someone who was practically a stranger to her was not an option.

She reached into the trunk of her car, pulled out two rolling suitcases from inside, and set them on the ground just as a large pickup truck slowly rolled past the driveway. Willa lifted her head up at the sound of the roaring engine, to see the passenger, a woman who she instantly recognized, with her piercing blue eyes and short dark hair, staring intently at her.

Willa's eyes widened with a nervous excitement and she started to raise her hand up to wave, until the driver, a man with matching blue eyes and dark hair, leaned forward in his seat to give a menacing glare directed at Willa. She sucked in and almost choked on her own breath.

The truck tires spun and they took off rapidly down the street and out of sight around the corner.

Willa slammed the back of her car shut and roughly ran her fingers through her curly hair before grasping at the back of her neck and kicking the tiny wheel of her suitcase. In a matter of a few seconds, every reason why she had never returned to Laurel Cove just crossed her path again and reminded her that she shouldn't be here now.

Chapter Two

*P*acking up the house in preparation for placing it on the market was too overwhelming to deal with right now, and her attempt at taking a nap was unsuccessful, so Willa made her way into the heart of the little town. She chose to walk the two miles, because she had always done it that way as a teenager, and taking a different route by car just seemed wrong. It would also make up for the fact that she missed her morning workout session due to her long drive to Maine.

The rows of tiny summer cottages intermingled with the few year round residential houses were just as she had remembered them. Strict regulations on development along the seacoast caused a lack of growth to the area, so she wasn't surprised at how everything seemed to have paused in time. It was refreshing for houses and buildings that reached a maximum of two stories in height to surround her. Skyscrapers surrounded the view from her apartment in New York City, which blocked out all views of nature, and left not just a grey backdrop, but also a dark void in her soul. Not a day passed when she yearned to be in the open, airy atmosphere of Laurel Cove.

Willa crossed the road and walked along the strip of businesses that bordered the sea. A narrow wooden walkway led to the back deck of a pub called The Anchor, where anyone who wasn't preparing their own food at home would go for a meal, and every lobsterman would stop by for a beer after ending a tiring day on the water.

The warm summer temperatures had the deck tables full, but Willa wanted to hide within the confines of the dimly lit bar anyway.

She caught a few people turning their heads, trying to get a glimpse of the woman who looked out of place, wearing designer clothing instead of what was available at the department store on the mainland, where the majority of the Cove residents shopped. The only other option was from a tiny consignment shop in which the same outfits got recycled from one generation to the next, until just about every family in the Cove had passed them around to the point of tearing at the seams.

It wasn't out of the ordinary for the occasional tourist to veer away from the beach or the gift shop, which were the common places to visit on the island, but only locals knew the back entrance to the pub. Willa managed to sneak in unrecognized because of how fast she passed through the deck area. Instead of stopping to take in the sights of the ocean water flowing just below the boards beneath her feet, or the rows of boats tied up along the docks, she averted her eyes down and kept moving. She knew her father's boat would be in view from the deck and that was something she had not mentally prepared herself for yet.

Thankfully, there was only one other person sitting at the bar and he looked too old and drunk to pay attention to Willa, but just to be sure, she took a seat as far away from him as possible. The bartender, a tall lanky woman with red hair, was setting a full glass of beer in front of him, so she was sure the drink would occupy him more than checking her out.

Willa didn't even have time to register in her mind who the bartender was, when a shrill voice cut across the bar. "Willa Barton, now there's a face I thought I'd never see again."

Willa sunk down in her barstool and did a quick sweep of the area behind her to find that no one was there to overhear the announcement of her name. If she had been in Los Angeles, cameras would have been thrust in her face and fans would be swooping in to get an autograph. Realizing how ridiculous she must look, Willa sat up in her seat and composed herself. It was then that she recognized the woman staring at her with her hands on her hips. "Oh, Meg, we all have to go back to where we started at some point in our lives, don't we?"

Megan leaned over the bar, spreading the upper half of her body across it to give a single armed hug and a kiss on the cheek to Willa. "Not if you become as successful as you have and can afford to stay away from the Cove."

"Success is just a matter of opinion."

Megan flashed Willa a doubtful look and waved her finger back and forth in an incriminating way. "Our busiest nights here are when we offer half price drinks every time your books hit the best seller list and two for one shots when your latest movie releases."

"Damn, you throw better parties than my publisher does for me."

Megan tossed the dishtowel she was using to dry off a glass over her shoulder and rubbed her hands together. "Your drinks are on the house tonight for all the times you missed out. What'll it be, the usual?"

A laugh unintentionally escaped from Willa.

"The usual? The last time we drank together, it was a random mixture of stolen liquor from our parents' cabinets."

"Do you think just because it's been twenty years that I can't remember the ingredients of the concoctions I came up with back then? How do you think I got my bartending skills?"

Willa smiled, happy with the playful banter between herself and someone who knew her before the rest of the world did. "My tastes have changed after years of attending cocktail parties and events. I'll take a glass of Cabernet Sauvignon please."

Megan set a wine glass down on the counter and poured it full for Willa. "Speaking of the big twenty, you're going to the reunion this Saturday, right?"

Willa twirled the red liquid around in her glass with a somber feeling building within her. "I'm only in town briefly to take care of my father's estate."

"Oh, I'm sorry, sweetie. I got so caught up in reminiscing that I forgot about your dad passing." Megan reached across the bar to place her hand on top of Willa's.

Willa nodded in appreciation for the comforting touch, but she thought quickly of something to say that wouldn't bring on the tears that so desperately wanted to fall. "I'm just glad his heart took him instead of the sea like so many other lobstermen have gone."

"He'll get his name up on the wall dedicated to those who made their living on their boats." Megan motioned to the wall at the far end of the bar. The names of men and even a couple of women were inscribed on tiny golden plates. Each one had a photo of them proudly next to their respective boat.

"I have the perfect picture for you." Willa took

a long sip of her drink. "Dad loved the water so much that he refused anything I offered to him in hopes that he would retire early."

Megan eyed the twenty-dollar bill Willa had placed on the bar when she wasn't paying attention. "Or maybe he was too stubborn to accept something given to him." She picked up the money, placed it in Willa's hand, and forced her to fold her fingers closed around it. "Stubborn like his daughter."

Willa smirked, appreciating that Megan could make the heaviness of the conversation lift into a more playful mood. During high school, Megan was always the optimistic one of the group, keeping them laughing even through finals week. It was no wonder why she ended up working at the local bar; socializing was her specialty.

The thick wooden door to the bar slammed shut, diverting Megan's attention to the most recent customer's needs. Willa took the opportunity to slip the twenty dollars into the glass tip jar on the counter.

Willa could hear the sound of rubber boots clomping on the hardwood floor behind her, causing the tiny hairs on the back of her neck to prickle out. When the man pulled out the stool two seats away from her, she shimmied to the far edge of her own stool and crossed her legs away from him. It wasn't as if he was right beside her, but he was still close enough to possibly initiate a conversation she didn't feel like starting, so she turned slightly in the opposite direction to avoid eye contact.

Megan popped the cap off a bottle of beer and set it down in front of the guy at the bar. Willa wondered if Meg ever even needed to ask anyone what they wanted. She then pictured herself stopping back in every night this week for another glass of wine until she was done with all the business she needed to complete in Laurel Cove.

Megan's voice broke through Willa's thoughts. "I know you'll be busy, but it would be fun to have someone to talk to at the reunion and I know a lot of people would love to see you there."

At the mention of the reunion, the man that Willa worked so diligently at evading turned his head and examined her through narrowed eyes. Willa could tell immediately upon a sideways glance who he was. Even with a face hidden behind a scruffy beard, and muscular stature obscured beneath a protruding beer gut, it was still easy to place him as her ex boyfriend's best friend. Willa thought she would chance it and offer up a friendly smile, although she was quite certain that Craig wouldn't fall for her false charm.

"Willa, huh? I'm pretty sure Griff won't be too happy about you showing up and ruining the party."

Willa opened her mouth to defend herself, but the words came at a loss to her. How could she possibly reply, when deep down, she believed he was right? She didn't want to attend anyway, and she had told Megan she wasn't going, so there was no point in bothering to convince him that she should.

Craig dug at the label of his beer bottle with a dirt-encrusted fingernail and peeled it off with a single tug. The sound of the paper tearing away from the glass made Willa's stomach turn. At the lack of a response, he leaned in closer towards Willa and she could feel the intimidation in his hot breath. Willa gulped down the last of her drink, her insides shaking with a nervous twitch. Thankfully, Megan stepped in and extended her arm across the bar to create a barrier between them.

"Griffin doesn't have a say as to who attends." She worked at diffusing the issue. "I'd like to think after all these years, we'd matured enough to drop old grudges," Megan reasoned as she removed Craig's empty bottle from the counter and slyly replaced it with a fresh one.

Willa had hoped he would back off and occupy himself with the drink, but instead, Craig pointed a dirty finger at her and gritted his teeth. "What she did to Brynn is unforgivable." Although he spat his words out in rage, a glimmer of sorrow passed over his face.

"Then that's for Brynn to decide, now isn't it?" Megan backed her guard up slightly, but maintained a close proximity. Even though he was double her size, she looked like she was prepared to pounce on the brute if need be.

"If Brynn was my sister, I'd feel the same way," he mumbled under his breath before downing half of the new bottle.

Megan shot Craig a warning glare, fit for an unruly child, before taking the time to uncork the wine bottle. "Well, there will be plenty of other people at the reunion to socialize with and the twins will just have to deal with it." Megan went to refill Willa's glass but Willa gently tapped on her hand and shook her head to refuse.

She stepped down from her barstool. "It's okay, Meg. Craig is right. It's best for everyone if I stay away." Her voice cracked with defeat.

"You know where to find me if you change your mind." Megan made a sweeping motion, encompassing the entire bar area.

Willa raised her hand to wave goodbye to Megan

before rushing out of the bar.

The entire walk home, Willa continuously looked over her shoulder in anticipation of Craig following and catching up to her. She assured herself that if anything, he would only dish out a verbal attack on her. Even though she believed her ex, Griffin, and his sister, Brynn, were the only ones that had a valid reason for the vendetta against her, she held onto the irrational idea that he still had a score to settle with her. Griffin and Craig had been teammates for nearly every sport in school and she assumed they were still just as close now as they had been then.

It wasn't until she locked herself into her father's house that she felt safe again.

Chapter Three

Willa settled back into her childhood bedroom like an old pair of jeans. Her father had done a meticulous job of keeping it dusted and clean while somehow not disturbing any of the objects from where she had last left them. She had never really considered what had become of her old room, but she figured that when she never returned after college, he would have turned it into something functional for himself, such as a den.

It was odd and yet strangely soothing for a time capsule of her youth to surround her. Sleep overcame her swiftly after a long and emotional day, but the same horrific nightmare that plagued her repeatedly throughout the last twenty years came again now.

An eighteen-year old Willa stood facing the edge of a swimming pool, mesmerized by the water sparkling on the surface from the lights lining the inside walls of the pool. Colorful strips of lights had been strung up above, giving a whimsical atmosphere to the backyard.

Brynn came bounding in from out of nowhere with her exuberant energy and stepped in front of Willa. Willa's face lit up with a giant smile as Brynn handed her a red plastic cup with who knew what sort of mixture of alcohol in it, but she took a giant gulp anyway and handed it back.

Despite Willa's attempt at letting loose and partying, Brynn had always been able to see beyond her outer layer and pinpoint her true feelings. "You've been quiet tonight."

Even Willa couldn't figure out what was off about that night. "I just can't believe it's really over."

"Over? Our lives are just starting now." *Brynn raised her cup above her head in triumph as if she just won another big game from the list of sports she played. Willa grinned at the enthusiasm of her best friend's attitude and playfully punched her arm. She had put what she thought was a good amount of power behind it, but Brynn barely noticed the tap to her well defined arm that was already quite tan despite summer just beginning. If it had been the other way around, Willa would be nursing a bruise to her arm by morning.*

"You know what I mean. We've all been accepted to different colleges. This is the last time all of us will be together." *Willa looked around the backyard of Brynn and Griffin's house, where mostly everyone from their graduating class was scattered about.*

"Our schools are only one state apart from each other. We can still meet up on weekends, right?" *Brynn was the one that looked concerned now, and Willa wondered if the same sense of loss was setting in with her too.*

Willa grabbed at the base of Brynn's shirt and twisted it in her hand with a tight grip, as if trying to hold onto what mattered most in her world. "Of course we will, and no matter where life takes us, you and Griffin will always be family to me."

"Griff will be on the other side of the country. Have you two talked about whether you'll stay together?"

Willa looked across to the opposite side of the pool where Griffin sat on top of a picnic table, laughing at something one of his friends had said. Being born only a few minutes apart from his twin, Griffin and Brynn couldn't possibly look any more alike than they did with their piercing blue eyes and shiny dark hair. When he noticed Willa was staring at him, he flashed a cocky grin, tossed the baseball in his hand up in the air, and made a show of catching it behind his back. "We haven't discussed it, but I think it goes unsaid that neither one of us wants to deal with a long-distance relationship. To be honest with you, I think he only asked me to be his girlfriend because he was afraid one of his obnoxious friends might try to date me."

Willa reached for Brynn's cup and took a long sip of the drink. When she went to hand it back to her, she swayed slightly and almost fell to the side. Brynn put a hand on Willa's waist to help steady her.

Brynn let out a deep throaty laugh. "Easy there. You do want to remember some of this night, don't you?"

"Ha, yeah." Willa grinned and ran a hand through her blond curls. She watched as Brynn's lips curled up into a slight smile at the simple motion she just made, but she caught a glimmer of sadness in her eyes as she looked down into her cup. "Hey, what's wrong?"

"There's something I've been wanting to tell you for a long time now, but I didn't want to hurt Griff. But, now that I know you two aren't planning on a future together, maybe I can finally stop hiding how I feel."

Willa's shoulders dropped in unease. She had never seen her friend open up about anything on an emotional level. Willa had been the one to express every thought in her mind out loud, but Brynn was the rock who seemed to float through adolescence so easily. "Please, Brynn, don't hold anything back."

Brynn took a step forward, closing what little space there already was between them, and placed one

strong arm around Willa's waist to pull their bodies
together. Willa wasn't sure what was happening until
she felt Brynn's lips press firmly against hers with a
surge of unsureness and need.

Willa's mind swirled with confusion and when
she opened her eyes, the view over Brynn's shoulder was
that of her boyfriend with an expression of pure rage.

Willa's arms extended straight out in front of her
with a power she never knew she had in her and pushed
directly into Brynn's chest. Willa had perceived them to
be closer to the pool than they were. The gut-wrenching
crack as Brynn's back hit the concrete edge of the pool,
followed by the sound of Brynn splashing into the water,
was always what woke Willa from the dream.

Willa sat upright in the small bed, grasping onto
the comforter with white knuckles. She couldn't tell if
the scream she heard was from someone in the dream
or a sound that she herself had just made. Her sweat
soaked T-shirt clung to her chest, so she tugged at the
collar in hopes that it would make it easier for her to
take a breath.

She reached out and spun the tiny knob a few
times to turn on the lamp on the nightstand. The light
from it cast a soft glow that illuminated a picture frame
sitting next to the lamp. She picked up the photograph
and stared down at it through tear-filled eyes. The
image that stared back at her was of Brynn and Griffin
both in their respective softball and baseball uniforms.
She sat between them, an arm around each of their
necks and a thick novel in her lap. It made a smile skirt
around her mouth amidst the sadness, to be reminded
of how a bookworm could find a companionship with
a couple of athletes. The bonds she shared with them
since elementary school had never been duplicated

with anyone in adulthood and it pained her to know she was the cause of severing their friendship.

Willa yearned for the night to come when she could stay in the dream just a little bit longer. The actual events that occurred after the deafening splash, all the way up until the next morning, were absent from her memory. There were flashes of images from the unaccounted for gap of time that came to her randomly, such as falling to her knees and feeling blood dripping down her face. She could also clearly recall Griffin jumping in and pulling Brynn's limp body out of the pool. The one thing that hurt the most and remained distinctly vivid in her mind, though, was Griffin's blood curdling yell towards her, to stay away from Brynn.

Willa dropped the photograph face down on the nightstand and rushed across the hall to the bathroom. She stood at the sink, with bare feet cold against the tile floor, and splashed water over her face, trying to wash away the visions. Her trembling hand turned the faucet off and after wiping the droplets of water away with a towel, she stared at the reflection of herself in the mirror. The last time she stood in here in this very same position, she had made a decision.

The two people that had mattered the most to her refused to see her, or so Griffin had made that clear every time she tried to visit the hospital. The others in her life didn't know what to think of Willa. Her father felt bad for her, but at the time was more worried about the potential legal ramifications of the incident, which Brynn thankfully declined bringing about. The rest of the small town spread rumors, which made Willa out to be a horrible drunk who cheated on her high school sweetheart and then tried to kill his twin sister. After a week of enduring the agony of being an outcast in her own town, Willa chose to run away from it all.

She left on a backpacking trip across the United States with nothing but a tent and a bag of necessities to survive the summer until college started in the fall. She kept a detailed account of her adventures in a journal, which ironically became the first of her published stories. Somewhere in the back of her mind, Willa questioned how her career would have been different had she not ventured out when she did, but regardless of what she had become, she still saw it as a cowardly way to escape. The possibility of having to come back to Laurel Cove someday constantly loomed above her head as her father aged, but she did not quite expect it to happen this soon.

Willa despised the fact that she had come here to settle her father's estate and yet her own past demons coming back to haunt her overshadowed the grieving. Her dad deserved to have this time from her without distraction and she would try her best to see to it that he did.

Preparing the house to be sold was one of the major projects she intended to complete while she was here and that meant cleaning everything out of it. While still standing at the bathroom vanity, she noticed his toothbrush sticking out of a mug with a sailboat on it. She pulled it out and held it over the small wastebasket beside the toilet. Her hand shook and instead of dropping it, she wrapped her fingers so tightly around the slender handle that her nails dug into the palm of her hand. A wave of disappointment washed over her when she recognized the level of anxiety she was experiencing over letting go of something so simple. Objects of value that would be a lasting tribute to his life filled the house, and yet she couldn't bring herself to dispose of a meaningless piece of trash. "Damn it," Willa cursed out loud as she stabbed the toothbrush back into the mug, rushed out of the room, and climbed back into her bed.

Two hours of consistent tossing and turning later, a frustrated Willa sat on the edge of the bed, staring at the red digital numbers of the alarm clock on her nightstand. She currently utilized a cell phone as her alarm, as most people did, but she found it amusing that her father must have had to change the batteries in this old thing so many times over the years to keep it running. She also pictured him coming in during daylight saving time to set it ahead or turn it back to maintain the correct time on it. He was playing the role of a father even if she wasn't around to need it.

Even with the lack of sleep from the previous night, it was evident her mind would not allow her to get some tonight either, so Willa picked up her laptop bag and made her way into the living room. She dragged the coffee table closer to the couch and sunk into the leather cushions, where she could comfortably spend the rest of the night getting lost in the world of her fictional characters.

Chapter Four

Willa woke up with her face plastered against the leather couch. She figured that, at some point during the night, she must have pulled down the knitted afghan that could always be found folded across the top of the couch, and covered herself with it. The afghan predated her lifetime, and she now wished she had asked her father if a family member had made it. She guessed that many questions would come up for her over the course of the next week and she was disappointed she hadn't cared to ask about things like that when she was young and living there. It seemed almost useless to hold onto something without a history to it and she hoped Aunt Beth would be able to help her sort through some of the important items.

Willa clicked on her laptop screen, which came out of sleep mode and informed her that she last saved her manuscript less than three hours ago. She sighed loudly at the realization that she only got an extended nap and not a full night of rest. The reflection staring back at her in the mirror moments later solidified that fact by showing off the dark lines under her eyes. She decided no amount of makeup could fix her sleep deprived face, so there was no point in trying to.

With so much to do around the house, she thought the best place to start would be her father's file cabinet, where the items could speak for themselves. She was fortunate that he only retained the most recent copies of bills and necessary paperwork, such as the title and deed to the house, boat, and vehicle. She wrote out checks to mail, covering his credit cards and utilities, leaving just a local one to stop by in person to pay off. Willa thought it would be best to go in person to the physician's office to pay the bill from her father's last physical, and to dispose of all the prescription medications in his bathroom cabinet properly.

On her way out the door, Willa considered taking her dad's truck, which she had not yet dared open the garage to see. It would be easier for her to fit in with all the locals instead of navigating the country roads in her sports car. Her hand wavered over the set of keys dangling from the hook next to the door, but then the thought arose that it was too soon to dredge up all the memories that would resurface from all the good times they had shared in the old truck. She grimaced at the idea of staying longer than she had planned because of her need to avoid emotional encounters.

She crossed the parking lot of the Cove Clinic and started up the steps to the front entrance, when a door closing on the side of the building caught her attention. She placed a hand on the side paneling and peered around the corner. Willa held her breath as she recognized the back view of the woman with short dark hair as she rolled down the wooden ramp that wound progressively downward to the ground. She was fast and almost reckless, yet skilled in her maneuvering around the corners. An exhilarating rush washed over Willa just by watching her, until it hit her that she was the cause of Brynn being confined to the wheelchair she was sitting in.

Willa turned away so that Brynn wouldn't catch her watching, and pushed her back against the railing for support. She sucked in air in frantic gasps as a wave of anxiety flowed through her. Just as she thought she was regaining her composure, images of Brynn being pulled from the pool would flash in her mind and it felt as though someone was choking her. She swiped at the exposed skin at her throat, realizing there wasn't anything constricting on it, except for her own perception of tightness closing in on her.

The glass door just inches away from Willa swung open and a woman dressed in scrubs stepped out. Willa tried to make her gasping breaths seem natural looking instead of the out of control mess that she knew was being projected to others. The woman didn't fall for her act and instead placed a calming hand on her arm.

"You should come inside and take a seat. The air conditioning will help you catch your breath a little easier."

Willa shook her head, not wanting to enter the waiting room area where everyone would surely gawk at her embarrassing episode. "No," she let out in a strangled voice.

The woman seemed to understand her reservations and did her best to reassure her. "It's okay; there's no one in the waiting area except for the receptionist." She held the door open, urging her in.

Willa reluctantly stepped into the little room and dropped down into the seat closest to the door. She wished that the woman hadn't noticed her and she could have made it back to her car, but now that she was in, everything in her body had begun to resolve itself. She wondered if it was due in part to the pastel paint on the walls, the soothing bubbles in the aquarium, and the lighthouse sculpture on the side table. The entire room was designed to give off a positive psychological response.

The woman in scrubs filled a paper cup with water and handed it to Willa, who nodded in appreciation and drank it down in a few gulps.

"Are you here to see Dr. Martin?"

"No, I just need to pay a bill," Willa explained as she dug for the envelope in her purse.

"I think that while you're here, you should at least talk to Dr. Martin about what just happened out there. It was a pretty severe panic attack."

Willa stared back at the woman with a confused look. "I was a patient of Dr. Martin for most of my childhood, but I'm quite sure that he's too old to be practicing still."

"You are correct. He retired a few years ago, but his daughter, Shannon Martin, took over his practice when he left."

"Would it be possible for me to just see you, since you witnessed what happened to me, that way I don't have to explain it to another person?"

"I'm the wrong kind of doctor. I'm a physical therapist."

"So, you must be Brynn's doctor?"

The woman looked at Willa apprehensively. "I perform therapy work for any patient that needs my services at this clinic."

Willa understood that she couldn't share that information with her. "Well, I guess that I'll take your advice and see the doctor."

"I think it's best that you do. Take care of that bill with Caroline at the desk and I'll let Dr. Martin know that you are waiting."

After filling out health history forms for ten minutes, Willa finally found herself sitting with her legs dangling off the side of an exam table with crinkling paper under her thighs. She was unaware of the tight grip she had on the leather straps of her purse, or how she was winding them around her fingers until the circulation was being cut off.

Shannon Martin sat on a rolling stool, entering the numbers from Willa's vital stats into the computer. Her brown hair was pulled up on the back of her head and it reminded Willa of when she used to sit behind her in algebra class. While Shannon had been fortunate enough to have the help of her father in the math and science classes, Willa studied relentlessly and came out overall as the class valedictorian because of excelling in English, which Shannon struggled with.

Shannon spun her seat around and scooted it in closer to Willa as she extended her hand out towards her. "It's good to see you again, Willa."

Willa unraveled her fingers from the straps to shake her hand. "You as well, Shannon."

"It's Dr. Martin while we're in here," Shannon corrected her. "In tight knit communities such as ours, I find that a clear distinction between social and professional settings is necessary."

"Yes, of course."

Shannon noticed the lifeline to her purse that Willa had created with the tangled mess between her fingers. She rolled over to her desk and searched through one of her drawers. When she returned to Willa, she gently removed the purse from her hands. "Let's set this aside for now and give you something a little less harsh on your fingers." Shannon placed a heart shaped piece of soft foam in Willa's palm.

The stress relief heart had a cute cartoon face printed on it as well as the Cove Clinic phone number and the advertisement for a prescription heart medication that Willa recognized from one of her father's pill bottles. She wondered how effective it was since it didn't prevent his heart attack from taking his life. When she squeezed the heart, it gave a satisfyingly squishy sensation in her hand, which helped to release some of the tension she was holding on to. "Thanks. I needed this."

Shannon nodded and moved on to review the numbers she had just entered into the computer. "Your pressure and pulse are a little higher than normal, but under the circumstance of what just happened to you, it's expected that they would be slightly elevated. Due to your family history, we should monitor them closely in the future."

"Will I have to be placed on medication for my heart someday, like my father was?"

"The chances are slim as long as you eat healthy and exercise. Your father was relentless with his meat and potatoes diet, and while lobstering may be laborious, it doesn't replace a workout."

Willa reached into her bag and pulled out the plastic baggie filled with tiny bottles. "By the looks of it, I don't think he actually even took any of these pills."

Shannon took the bag and sifted through the contents of it with a concerned look on her face. "You're right." She tossed the bag up on the counter behind her.

"If he had taken them, do you think he might still be alive now?"

"I never like to play the *what if* scenario where people's lives are concerned, but let this be a lesson to remember with your health and what changes you need to make now."

"I have better eating habits than he did and I do a cardio workout daily at the gym when I'm in New York."

"Good, that's what I like to hear. So, do you regularly suffer from panic attacks?"

"No, never."

"Do you know what might have triggered the one you just had? Stress resulting from the death of a loved one is definitely a cause to bring one on, even if you've never experienced it before."

"While my father's death *has* been an emotional roller coaster, I can't blame my panic attack on that." She squeezed the foam heart in her fist until portions of it protruded out from between her fingers. "This whole thing was brought on because I saw Brynn when she was leaving the building." Willa didn't need to explain anything else about the situation. She knew that Shannon was present the night of the incident and she was grateful that she wouldn't have to relive the events of that moment out loud to someone all over again.

Shannon took on a solemn expression as she thought. "Would you be willing to see a different doctor, one that has more professional experience in this field of study?"

"You mean a psychologist instead of a physician?"

"Yes."

"I've lost count of how many sessions with psychologists, psychiatrists, and counselors that I attended over the years in an attempt to resolve the guilt I have for what I've done, but I don't feel comfortable seeing someone in this small town where I most likely also know the therapist."

"I can understand that. How about if I prescribe

you something that will at least help you sleep at night?" Shannon motioned to Willa's eyes. "It looks as though you've been having some problems with that lately, am I right?"

"That would be helpful, thank you, Dr. Martin."

Shannon handed a piece of paper to Willa with the prescription written on it and helped her down off the exam table. "If you need to see me again while you are in Laurel Cove, don't hesitate to schedule an appointment."

Just before stepping out into the hallway, Willa turned to Shannon. "Can I ask you one more thing?"

"Of course."

"Is there any possible chance of Brynn walking again?"

Shannon placed a soothing hand on Willa's forearm. "You know I can't break the confidentiality of any of my patients. That is a question you will just have to ask her yourself."

"I can't do that."

"Have you spoken to her at all since that night?"

Willa focused on the pattern in the tiles on the floor and shook her head. "No."

"I think you should try. She's asked me about you in the past because she knew that we went to college in the same state. She thought that maybe we kept in touch."

Willa's heart fluttered at the idea that Brynn asked about her, but she pushed that thought aside, not wanting to hope for something that might not exist. Brynn could have been asking out of spite, angry that Willa had the opportunity to fulfill her dreams of going off to school. She decided to deflect the subject back to Shannon. "I'm surprised that you ended up practicing here after going to Columbia University. I mean, you literally could have worked anywhere in the world."

"It wasn't my intention to come back to Laurel Cove at first, but when my dad announced his retirement, I felt a sense of duty to take over the clinic that my grandfather originally started. I'm glad I did now, because there's something charming about this little community and the people in it. Speaking of which, you *will* be at the reunion tomorrow night, right?"

"I've already decided that it's probably best if I don't go."

"If you did, it would be the perfect opportunity to ask a certain someone the question that you asked me."

"That's reason enough for me to stay away. You've already seen what happens to me just from seeing her from a distance."

"Or the direct encounter could provide the therapy that you've been needing all along."

"I don't know about that theory, but maybe I'll see you there."

Chapter Five

The prescribed medication to help Willa sleep worked a little too effectively. She woke up late in the afternoon, still in her clothes from the day before, glasses pressed to her face, and computer screen open and glowing on the coffee table. She sat up with a groggy feeling in her head and stomach growling.

Willa decided that tonight she would actually eat something before taking one of the pills and only take half the dose to avoid waking up to another morning like this again. Now that she stopped to think about it, she couldn't really remember having a full meal since the day before she left New York. Coffee, alcohol, and random snacks did not do the trick to replace her usual diet of nutritional food and she was famished just thinking about it. She scoured the refrigerator, cupboards, and pantry for something to eat, but soon realized that everything in the house required some resemblance of cooking skills in order to create a meal out of it. Her father had been an excellent home chef, but she had never acquired the skills from him because he insisted that it was his duty as a single parent to provide for her. College meal plans were included with her tuition scholarship, and restaurants and delivery options saturated New York, so the need never arose for her to have to cook.

The only place in Laurel Cove to get a quality meal was The Anchor. If she started walking now, she would have time to eat a sandwich before the lobstermen ended their day, so she wouldn't have to worry about crossing paths with Craig again. Another gorgeous day out meant that the deck would be packed with a Saturday crowd and the inside of the bar would be safe from possible interactions with people.

Sure enough, when Willa stepped into The Anchor, the only other person inside was the same old man at the end of the bar. She pulled one of the menus off an empty table and took it with her to the counter, where she sat in the same seat as last time. Less than a minute later, Megan pushed through the door from the kitchen area and bounded over to the bar. "I had a feeling you'd show up today. Did you change your mind about tonight?" Megan asked with a giant grin on her face.

Willa glared at the overly excited Megan through heavily lidded eyes. "Take it down a notch, Meg. I'm just here for some lunch."

She could feel the scrutiny as Megan took in the current state of her appearance. Willa hung her head over the menu, pretending to be occupied with a decision, although the menu hadn't changed at all from how she remembered it. She was all too aware of the fact that her wavy hair was a disheveled mess that a hair tie couldn't even tame, and her clothes were riddled with wrinkles, obviously because she had slept in them.

"Oh honey, you had a rough night, huh? Don't worry, I can fix you up with a good meal, and that will give me plenty of time to talk you into making a grand appearance at the school tonight."

"Ugh, if you say it like that, I definitely won't go. I want to remain as unnoticed as possible." Willa rested the weight of her head in her hands. "Is the reunion really going to be held at the high school?"

"Of course. Where else would they be able to fit us all in one place in this town? They wouldn't spring for the cost of renting a location for us to use."

"I'll take the club sandwich with an orange juice, and you're going to have to do a much better job of trying to talk me into going, because it just keeps sounding worse by the minute."

Megan jotted down the order on a pad of paper and delivered it to the kitchen staff before returning to the bar. She filled a glass of water with ice and handed it to Willa. "There must be some people that you want to reconnect with after all these years."

Willa shrugged. "It was nice talking to both you and Shannon again."

"You're referring to *Dr. Martin*, right?" Megan exploded with laughter. "I told her that just because she went to school for eight more years than I did, so that she'd be qualified to stick a plastic tube in my private parts, does not mean that I'm going to stop calling her by the name she had written on her desk in kindergarten, sitting next to me."

Willa joined her in laughter, and by the time her stomach was hurting from bursting with happiness, she was already feeling the effects of the medication easing out of her system. "Shannon said that I should go tonight too," Willa mentioned after the giggles subsided.

"Well, there, you have the recommendation from a doctor. If a bartender can't convince you, listen to the professional."

"Let's say that I did decide to go. I didn't really pack anything appropriate to wear for the occasion."

"Oh please, you're from New York City. Your pajamas are more glamorous than my Sunday best, and you have to admit that half the guys there will walk in wearing flannel shirts and smelling like lobster bait." Again, the two women erupted into belly rolling laughter that echoed off the walls of the bar.

Megan took off behind the kitchen door and came back balancing a tray with a plate of food and fresh squeezed orange juice. Willa reached for a fry before the dish could make it out of Megan's hand. "I should just open up a tab for the week, because I know that I'll be eating here a lot."

"Are you planning on staying for a while?"

"At least until I get my father's house ready to put on the market, and at the rate I've been going, it might take longer than I expected."

"If there's anything I can do to help, just ask."

Willa felt her chest get tight in a way that it would when sadness started to creep in, but this time she felt as though feeling like someone genuinely cared for her brought it on. Sure, there were people in her life that she knew would come to her rescue if she called on them to help her out, but most of them were acquaintances in the book or film industry who relied on her creativity for their own careers to thrive. She couldn't help but wonder if they would be so quick to help her if she weren't supporting their paychecks. This woman in front of her, though, was willing to offer her time and support without anything in return, and that meant more to Willa than she could ever begin to express. "I wish we had been closer friends back when we were in school." Willa tried to hide the emotions welling up in her eyes by adjusting the layers in her sandwich so that they stacked up perfectly before taking a bite.

"Let's make a fresh start tonight, back at the same building where it all began. Of course, this time I won't need to bribe you to write my English papers for me."

Willa nearly choked on her orange juice. "I almost forgot. You tried to offer me rides home on that old rusty electric scooter for a month, in exchange for a five-page paper."

"Hey, it was a good deal, at least until Griffin and Brynn found out about it. How was I supposed to know that they'd be so insistent on walking you home from school every day?"

Willa felt overcome with loss as she looked back on all those years of walking home with the Reed twins through the sun, rain, and snow. Her favorite memory was in the pouring rain with Griffin carrying her backpack while she and Brynn huddled under an umbrella together. Despite their efforts, all three of them were drenched by the time they reached Willa's house. Her dad had mugs of hot cocoa waiting by the fireplace for them when they stumbled in, dripping wet. She came out of the daydream, realizing that Megan was still staring at her, waiting for a response back. "Yeah, we'd been doing that ever since middle school." She took a bite of her sandwich. "I heard Griffin put an end to your offer."

"You were nice enough to help me with the paper anyway, but no, it wasn't Griffin. Brynn approached me in the parking lot and told me that there was no way she'd ever allow you on the back of my scooter. If I remember correctly, she referred to it as a *death trap on wheels.*"

Willa smiled as she tried to picture the more docile and laid back one of the twins, being protective of her. She closed her eyes for a moment as she slowly chewed the last bite of her meal, in hopes that Megan would leave her alone for a little while to reflect on the new angle of the memory that she had always perceived so differently in the past. Her assumption must have been correct about Megan's ability to read people and recognize that she needed some space, because Megan stepped aside to wipe the bar clean even if it didn't need it, and to refill the old man's beer. By the time that Willa was ready to talk again, it was getting dangerously close to the time that Craig might show up, so she pulled out her wallet from her purse to pay her bill.

Megan rushed over and placed a hand over Willa's to stop her from taking out the money. "I thought we had a plan to keep an open tab for you while you're in town?"

"Sure, if that's okay. It won't get you in trouble with your boss, will it?"

Megan's face lit up with a giant grin. "I am the boss. I bought out the original owner a few years ago when he opened a new place in Portland."

Willa looked at Megan with a nod of pride. "Good for you. This place has the most history in the Cove. I'm glad that it's in the hands of someone who will honor it well." Willa dropped her wallet back in her purse. "We will definitely be seeing a lot of each other this week then," Willa added as she stepped down from the barstool.

"That doesn't sound very hopeful for you planning on going with me tonight." Megan added a pouting lip to her conclusion.

Willa let out a deep breath as she seriously considered what she should do. "I'm scared about how Griffin will react to me being there."

Megan contemplated Willa with a concerned expression. "Are you sure it's not Brynn that you're really worried about?"

Willa's face scrunched up in a grimace as she held back the pain she had been attempting to conceal. She bobbed her head up and down when the words didn't come out fast enough. Then they escaped from her lips in a whisper, "Yes, I believe you're right about that."

Megan threw the towel she was holding down on the counter and made her way around to the other side of the bar. She stood in front of Willa and placed a grounding hand on either one of her shoulders until Willa lifted her head to make eye contact.

"You need to do this, for both you and Brynn. I promise that I won't leave your side while we're there unless you want me to, okay?"

Willa reluctantly nodded in agreement. "Thank you, Meg."

Chapter Six

Willa left the bar feeling mildly unconfident in the choice she made at the last minute to join Megan at the reunion. Sure, she had thought almost nonstop about it over the past two days, but the fears she had about going far outweighed the reasons why she wanted to be there. The idea crossed her mind that she could always come up with a valid excuse to cancel; she was still grieving the loss of her father, after all. Although, the idea of letting a very excited Megan down seemed to be a much worse consequence than anything that might possibly happen at the party.

The best course of action, she decided, was to ease herself slowly into the concept of seeing Brynn again. The Laurel Cove High School gymnasium was quite large, but there was a huge possibility that they would see each other at least from a distance. Willa didn't want a repeat of yesterday's panic attack in front of anyone, especially Brynn. If she could somehow see Brynn without interacting with her, then maybe she could control her emotions better when facing her in person.

Griffin and Brynn's mother, Jackie, owned the fitness center on the island, Mussels by the Sea. Willa's father had informed her that years ago, Jackie moved to Florida, like most of the retired Maine residents seeking warmer weather in their later years. The twins had taken over the business in her place. Mussels was a state of the art workout facility both inside and out, equipped with an indoor pool and outside ball courts overlooking the ocean. Many of the residents of Laurel Cove had a membership just to have access to the private beach on the fitness center's property. If there were one place that Willa might possibly get a glimpse of Brynn, it would be there.

Willa started walking in the direction of the gym, thankful that she had ventured into town by foot instead of taking her car, which would be easily recognized on a road rarely used by anyone not traveling there specifically to use the gym. As Willa wandered further down the cove, land filled with tall trees separated the distance between the houses. The architecture of the houses became more elaborate as well as larger, and exclusively summer residents owned many of them.

As she passed by one of her favorite houses on the road, a tall one constructed of stone with a widow's peak rising up in the back, she was brought back to a time when she used to stop in front of it with the twins. They would make plans to come back to the island with fortunes amassed after college and careers launched, then they would pitch in to buy the gigantic house to live in together. This memory hit Willa like a punch in the gut. She had done exactly as her dreams planned out, and could easily purchase any one of the homes along the cove, but her friends were lost to her and that hurt more than any amount of money could fix. The remainder of the walk became a bittersweet flashback of memories as she recalled every twist and turn of the road where conversations took place, hands were held, and songs were sung aloud.

When she rounded the bend where the tall wooden sign with Mussels by the Sea engraved into it came into view, Willa paused behind the trunk of a thick oak tree to observe the yard. Griffin's pickup truck, which she recognized from the other day, was parked in the lot, but he was nowhere to be seen. From the looks of it, the building had expanded in size since she had last been in it. The interior of the fitness center had been comprised of multiple rooms, and she was sure that he would be wherever the weightlifting equipment would be located. Another major difference was that the parking lot was now paved and there was a concrete ramp leading up to the front door at the entrance to the building. It brought a wave of nausea to Willa to think that she was the reason why those changes took place.

She stood in the same spot for many minutes while surveying the activity around the gym. Her hands, supported against the tree, were now sticky with sap and had imprints from the bark marking her palms. Every now and then, someone would walk by the large windows in the front of the building, but she was too far away from the building to recognize the silhouettes that passed.

Just as she was about to give up, Willa picked up on a sound that was out of place. Between the crashing of the waves on the shore, there was a consistent pounding beat like a ticking clock but with longer pauses spaced out in between at times. Willa followed the tree line to stay just out of sight, but made her way to the other side of the fitness center building. The wide-open space was sectioned off with wire fences for basketball courts and tennis courts. The pounding sound was coming from the tennis court where Brynn was playing against another woman.

Willa found a spot to settle in unseen behind

a row of pine trees. From this point, she was able to observe Brynn, who was fast in her wheelchair, able to spin on a moment's notice to hit the ball from every possible angle. Brynn's muscles protruded from under the straps of her tank top as she stretched the racket out to reach the ball. She had been strong back in her high school years compared to the other girls, but now she had matured into a perfectly sculpted body that mesmerized Willa. She couldn't help but keep her eyes glued to Brynn's biceps that glistened with sweat in the heat.

For the most part, Brynn's back was to Willa, but with every spin that she made, Willa held her breath, wondering if that would be the moment when Brynn might catch sight of her. It never happened, of course, because as in all things sports related with Brynn, her eye was always on the ball. Nothing else surrounding Brynn mattered but the game. Willa never cared much for sports, but watching either of the Reed twins in their element made the mundane act of a game exhilarating to her.

The tennis match stopped briefly as the woman who Brynn was playing against put her hands on her knees to catch her breath. Brynn used that time to wipe her brow with the band on her wrist, but she was practically bouncing with energy in her wheelchair and ready to continue. Her tennis partner went to the corner of the court, rolled out a machine to take her place, and turned it on before walking away. The machine shot out perfect serves to Brynn and Willa once again found that she couldn't help but be enthralled by the pure strength that emanated from Brynn.

Just when Willa started to come to terms with the idea that she might possibly be able to handle being at the same event with her old friend, a shout broke through the serenity of the moment. "Did you really think that no one would see you hiding there like some sort of creepy stalker?"

Willa spun around to see the woman who had been playing against Brynn on the court. She had been so focused on Brynn that the other person hadn't mattered to her, but now that she was closer, Willa immediately recognized her as Cassidy, a former teammate of Brynn's for multiple sports in their school days. Cassidy now stood with her tall, yet stocky stature in front of Willa, causing her to back up towards the direction of the courts and out from the cover of the trees.

"I was just watching you play, that's all."

"There were rumors of you being back, but you have no right to be *here* of all places. Stay away from her."

Another voice rang out from behind Willa and it made her jump to hear it.

"Cass, it's okay. Leave her alone."

Cassidy discovering her was one thing, but the embarrassment of Brynn catching them during their altercation made Willa take off in a rush to escape. She breezed by Cassidy and didn't slow down until she reached the end of the road. With every step, she thanked herself for the decision to slip on her running shoes that morning. By the time she finally came to a stop and looked down at herself, with wrinkled clothing, sap covered hands, and messy curls falling around her face, she wondered what Brynn must have thought about the disaster that she represented both outside and in.

The remainder of the walk back to the house

gave Willa too much time to analyze the interaction between Cassidy and Brynn. Cass had been Brynn's other half in all things sports related. In softball, they were pitcher and catcher, in basketball they were center and forward, and in soccer they were the strikers. Willa had spent all of her afternoons watching either Brynn or Griffin in some sort of sporting event, but she was always the one cheering them on from the bench. She was way too awkward when it came to physical games and preferred to be a spectator, often times with her face buried in a book while in the stands. Even after Willa and Griffin became a couple, she sometimes found that she was ever so slightly jealous of the teammate bond that Cass and Brynn had on the field or court. There were moments after an all-out battle in overtime when they would run to each other in elated exhaustion and embrace in an almost painful display of clashing together, which Willa secretly wished she could be a part of.

Seeing that Cass was still playing sports with Brynn twenty years later was frustrating enough, but to have Cass get in her face to defend Brynn was just plain insulting. Willa began to get angry with herself for missing out on years of friendship with Brynn while her competition had apparently never left, and most likely took her place for the title of best friend. As this thought crossed her mind and others took form, Willa stopped dead in her tracks. Could it be possible that Brynn and Cassidy were a couple now?

Willa kicked at the gravel on the side of the road in envy and then just as quickly, got mad at herself for getting upset about that idea. She should want happiness for her friend whose life she had destroyed in a drunken state that would haunt her for the rest of her life. Cass had been there to support Brynn for every catch, pass, and save for all the games they played and it only made sense that she be there for her as a romantic partner as well. She attempted to come to terms with the likelihood of Brynn and Cass being together as she finished her walk back to the house, but it just left her feeling irritated. Stepping into the house filled with the scents of her childhood long past gave her a different kind of sadness to revel in and she couldn't decide which one hurt more right now.

Life in New York was so much simpler in a hectic sort of way. She could get lost in a sea of people who really only cared about what everyone else thought about their latest fashion trends and how much their car cost. Willa could hide away from anyone who could recall her past and yet a crowd of unknown faces who loved her for the stories she wrote could adore her. At this moment, Willa wanted more than anything to trade all the sadness that Laurel Cove offered her for the emptiness that New York provided her.

The sailboat clock hanging on the living room wall showed that Willa had just a few hours to prepare herself for the night that she had promised to Megan. If she was going to do this, Willa decided that she would go all out for the event. She was going to attack this reunion as if she were attending a red-carpet Hollywood premier.

Chapter Seven

illa knocked on the heavy wooden door of the apartment above The Anchor. It was an identical match to the door that opened into the bar below. The silver knocker on the door was in the shape of an anchor, which matched the nautical theme of nearly every business and home décor item on the entire island. When she was young, Willa was tired of the ocean adornments constantly surrounding her, but when she was away from it, she found herself inadvertently buying lighthouse magnets when she came across them in gift shops.

The door opened and an auburn haired teenage girl looked at Willa with raised eyebrows before stepping aside to give her room to enter the apartment. "Mom is still getting ready." The girl, who was the spitting image of Megan when she was the same age, pointed out where to go before taking her place back down on the couch. She shoved a handful of microwave popcorn into her mouth as she stared up at an action movie blaring on the television.

Willa glanced at the screen out of the corner of her eye as she passed by and smiled, because she had adapted the film to a screenplay from a book that she had written. She had done that project many years ago and she was delighted to see that a new generation was still getting enjoyment out of it.

She made her way through the tiny, but well

taken care of apartment, to the open bathroom door where Megan was concentrating on applying mascara to her eyelashes. "I hope you don't mind. I showed up a little early."

Megan completed the finishing touches to one eye before turning to acknowledge Willa in the doorway, but when she did, her jaw practically dropped to the floor. "Oh, my God!"

Willa looked down at herself and then back up at Megan. "Too much?"

Megan couldn't take her eyes off Willa in her full-length evening gown that hugged every curve of her tall body. One side was split open from her ankle up to her thigh, allowing every step she took to reveal one entire leg. The strapless dress dipped down low on her chest, showing off her cleavage. It also left most of her back exposed, but her long hair hung down to cover it. Strung around her neckline was an elegant set of pearls adorned with delicate white gold settings and intermingled with diamonds that were strategically situated between every third, perfectly rounded pearl. "Let's just say, if I wasn't attracted to men, we would already be in my bedroom."

Willa let out a laugh that nearly choked her because of how form-fitted the dress was, especially in the stomach area. "Hey, wait, wouldn't I get any say in the matter?" she asked when she could finally breathe again.

Megan shook her head. "Not when you come in my house looking like that."

"I figured that tonight was an all or nothing situation. There are going to be a lot of people that won't be happy with me being there, so I might as well look good while being publicly shamed."

Megan peeled her eyes away to finish putting on her makeup. "You made a good choice. I don't think I could start a confrontation with anyone in that dress, even if it was my ex-husband wearing it."

After meeting a daughter in the living room and hearing about an ex-husband, Willa realized that she didn't know anything about Megan's life except for recently finding out that she owned The Anchor. Willa's life was an open book that a simple search on the internet could research. At any given time, fans would know what project she was currently working on, where she was vacationing, whom she was dating, and creepily, sometimes what she even had for lunch that day. Megan had been so supportive of all Willa's problems she was dealing with, but Willa was too caught up in her own issues that she didn't take the time to check in on Megan's life. She genuinely didn't want to make this into a one-sided friendship, so she decided to work on catching up, starting now. "So, the miniature version of you in the living room called you mom."

"Ava spoke to you, huh? It's just because I took the phone that's usually eight inches from her face away from her."

"Now she's sitting in front of a bigger screen," Willa observed, not understanding the punishment process that some parents chose for their children. "Did she come from this ex-husband you were referring to?"

"Yup. It turned out that he couldn't handle it out on a boat, so he sold his soul to the military. Apparently, he liked it so much that he chose not to come back for his family when he was done putting his time in."

"I'm sorry; that's horrible. Do you miss him?"

"Not anymore. I was twenty-three when I got pregnant, we got married at twenty-four, and divorced by twenty-seven. I've had plenty of time to get over him."

"So, you're not with anyone now?"

"At this point, I figure I may as well wait a few more years until she's out of the house." Megan used her tube of lipstick to motion towards her daughter in the living room. "This place is barely big enough for the two of us anyway. And besides, the tips are always larger for a bartender if they think you're single."

"You're right about that; I always leave more money if I think I have a chance of taking home my bartender," Willa teased, giving a playful wink to Megan.

"Ha ha," she sarcastically responded to Willa. "And speaking of tips, by the way, you need to stop leaving them for me. We're friends, and I don't want you to feel as though you have to do that."

"I have no idea what you're talking about," Willa said, with a guilty smirk playing at her lips.

"Hmm, it's a little obvious when you leave and I find a fifty-dollar bill in the tip jar."

"The old man at the end of the bar can be pretty sneaky when you're not looking."

They both broke out into another fit of laughter before Megan slid past Willa. "Let's get out of here."

When they stepped out into the parking lot of The Anchor, Megan reached into her purse to dig out a set of keys. Willa covered up her hand to stop her. "Don't worry. I've got transportation covered for the night."

Megan scanned the parking lot, which pickup trucks, all belonging to the usual customers, filled.

"Where's your car?"

"Our ride is waiting out front."

Megan scrunched up her face in a questioning look, but followed Willa around to the front of the building. As they turned the corner, a long, black, stretch limousine came into view, parked along the sidewalk. When Megan noticed it, she stopped and reached out for Willa's wrist as if she needed to feel grounded to make sure that what she was seeing was real. "No way. Is that for us?"

"What kind of party would it be if we can't both get a little inebriated?"

The limo driver, dressed in a suit just as pristine as the freshly waxed car, stood next to the door at the rear of the vehicle until Willa started walking towards it, then he promptly opened the door with a white glove, to usher her in with an offer of his hand. Megan took her time approaching the car and peered into it with wide eyes, taking in the view of the interior before slowly stepping inside and sliding her way down the length of the leather seat until she was across from Willa.

"I can't believe you rented a limo."

"It was a little difficult to get one in Maine on such short notice, but I didn't feel like crushing into the back seat of a cab wearing this." Willa pointed out the uncomfortable position she had to sit in to accommodate the dress. "Especially since we're picking up one other person."

"Who?"

"Shannon." Willa observed Megan's reaction for an indication of her approval because she had forgotten to ask if it was okay to invite her to join them. Megan seemed preoccupied with figuring out the controls to the sunroof and it was impossible for Willa to read her mood. "Is that all right with you?"

Megan's face lit up when she hit the right button that activated the roof to slide open, and the sky came into view. "I don't know Shannon very well besides from my yearly exam and the occasional fix up that my kid needs, from doing hell knows what in gym class. She rarely eats at the restaurant so I haven't had much of a chance to interact with her, but from what I've experienced, she's a kind person that I can't wait to get to know better."

"I'm glad. I kind of get the feeling that I'm going to need as many people on my side as I can get going into this reunion."

Megan flashed Willa an understanding smile and nod. "There sure is plenty of space to hold a party in here if we need to run away from whatever we face tonight."

Willa gave Megan a wink from across the aisle. "Now you know the real reason why I rented this thing."

The ride to Shannon's house didn't take too long, but it was challenging for the driver to take some of the curving back roads with a stretch limo. Willa made a mental note to give him an extra bonus at the end of the night. Before long, the slow, sharp turn before the limo came to a stop signaled that they had reached their destination.

Megan stood straight up in the center of the car and put her head up through the opening in the roof. She spun her entire body from one side to the other and then let out an excited gasp. Her fingertips reached out in Willa's direction and started to flap up and down rapidly. "You have to see this!"

Willa stood, which was difficult to do in a low

space, wearing a dress that didn't leave much room to move in, and wearing high heels that sunk into the fabric carpeting on the floor of the car. She had to shuffle her way over to Megan and then lean right up against her to allow them both to fit their heads up through the sunroof.

Shannon had texted her address to Willa and then she in turn provided it to the transportation company for an itinerary for the night, but she had been in such a hurry to get ready, that she didn't pay much attention to the address that she had been given. One of the most scenic roads in Laurel Cove wound all the way up the coastline, and a row of very fortunate properties along this stretch had the best views of the ocean from their backyards. Shannon's house was one of the lucky few to be located there. The two women stood with their heads poking out of the roof of the limo, taking in the marvelous scenery, until Willa became self-conscious of their gawking. She nudged Megan's side with her elbow. "Come on; let's be proper guests and go to her door."

Moments later, they both stood on the doorstep and rang the bell. Megan had a strange look on her face as she studied Willa's dress and then contemplated her own. "I'm really hoping that Shannon isn't wearing white when she answers that door."

Willa had a confused look on her face until she caught on to what Megan was referring to. "Oh, damn!" Laughter spilled out of both of the women. "I never imagined that we should have coordinated our outfits with one another!"

The door swung open before Willa and Megan had a chance to control their giggles. Shannon had a nervous smile on her face, not knowing how to interpret the situation she just walked in on. Willa quickly inspected the charcoal grey pantsuit outfit that Shannon was wearing and gave her forearm an assuring squeeze to show that they were in no way making fun of her.

Megan was the first to subside from their bout of sidesplitting laughter. "I just brought it to Willa's attention that it would be horrible if you happened to be wearing white tonight."

Shannon looked from Willa's blue dress and then to Megan's red one and then she too had a huge smile spread from ear to ear. "Oh my, we'd never hear the end of that joke, would we?" She stepped out and was about to close the door behind her, when she noticed that Megan was peeking into her house. "Would you like to come in for a minute before we go?" she offered.

Megan nodded enthusiastically and Willa found it amusing just how much she enjoyed every new experience she was having this evening, through the eyes of someone who obviously did not venture out of her own element very often. Willa had found it refreshing to see Megan's excitement over new things in her own environment. She couldn't help but wonder what it would be like to invite her to New York City for a completely different change of scenery. Maybe Megan could help her find the beauty hidden in the bleak backdrop of the skyscrapers.

No view could ever compare to the one they were taking in now, as the three women stood on the back patio, looking out over the rocky coast of the Atlantic Ocean. The stones that made up the patio were laid out in lavish geometric patterns with polished rock almost too exquisite to be walking on. The furniture, which consisted of a table, chairs, flower planters, a garden swing, and a bench, were all constructed out of driftwood. In the very center of the patio was a fire pit covered over with a grill to cook on.

"You must have some amazing gatherings out here," Megan commented.

Shannon made a sour face and winced as if the statement hurt. "More like a lot of lonely nights with myself, a book, and a glass of wine."

Megan raised her eyebrows in surprise. "That sounds like such a waste for a grill like this." She ran her fingers along the pristine metal surface that appeared to be hardly ever used.

"Maybe tomorrow night, the two of you could come over for dinner and drinks?" Shannon asked shyly. Apparently, her strong professional demeanor didn't carry over into her personal life.

"I could really use a relaxing evening like that," Willa said with a sigh.

Megan's eyes widened when the idea hit her. "I can bring over some steaks from The Anchor's kitchen to throw on the grill."

Willa smiled as a sense of peace settled over her. She was delighted with the prospect of spending time with people who didn't care about what designer's name she was wearing, or if she'd make her next deadline on time. She almost wished that they could just stay out here on the patio tonight too, away from all the critical voices she was bound to encounter at the school, but with these two women by her side, she was as prepared as she'd ever be.

Chapter Eight

The limousine rounded into the Laurel Cove High School parking lot just as the three women were taking their last sips from their glasses of champagne. Willa had the driver stock up the car with a few bottles before he picked them up. When he opened the door and shuffled aside to let them out, they were in the middle of a conversation about how none of them had even taken a limo to their senior prom. All of their dates took more pride in washing and waxing their muddy trucks for the night, instead of spending their money on an expensive luxury. One at a time, they slid out of the car with the help of the driver's white gloved hand and made their way to the front doors of the school.

Willa worked at masking how on edge she was with a timid grin, but Megan must have recognized the nervous look on Willa's face and decided to break the silence of the parking lot with a joke. "An author, a doctor, and a bartender walk into a high school gymnasium. I can only guess how this night will end up. I'm glad we started drinking on the way over here." Willa sucked in a deep breath, feeling as though she had an army standing by her side, with two highly supportive woman surrounding her.

As they started making their way down the halls of the school, Shannon scrunched up her nose. "That's one thing I don't miss, the odor of every adolescent boy in town condensed in one building."

Willa pulled a bottle of perfume from her purse, sprayed it into the air in front of them, and waved her hand to spread the fresh scent around. She held the bottle up to the fluorescent lights flickering above them and attempted to judge how much liquid was left in the tiny vial. "Hopefully there's enough in here to get us through the night without gagging."

A long table was set up at the entrance to the gym and the class vice president, Valerie, was sitting in a folding chair, handing out nametags. It was obvious when they approached her that she was not happy about being assigned the duty of greeting people all night. "Step up, ladies, and search for your own names. They're in alphabetical order. A diploma from here should make you more than capable of figuring it out for yourselves."

Shannon and Megan found their nametags and successfully pinned them to their outfits, but Willa grabbed hers and whispered a request to Valerie. "Can I change the name on my tag?"

Valerie wasn't so discrete in her response back as she bellowed it for everyone to hear. "We sent out request forms for nametag changes in our RSVP envelopes. If you chose not to send it back along with the invitation, you get whatever name you were enrolled into the school as." She narrowed her eyes and glared at Willa. "As I recall, you never bothered to respond to the event at all, so you're lucky that we're even allowing you in."

She decided to ignore the insane comment regarding the invitation. "Seriously, the letters are written on here with a black marker, just let me rub it off and borrow your marker to fix it."

Valerie glared back at Willa. "I don't care who you are; the rules are the rules and you have to follow them just like everyone else." Valerie wrapped her claw like, too long fingernails around the marker and set it in her lap.

A plastic bin on the corner of the table held a few supplies that were used in setting up the decorations for the event. Willa noticed a roll of duct tape sitting on the very top of the bin. Valerie eyed her suspiciously, but before she could react, Willa reached out and snatched the roll of tape from it. Valerie made a grunting sound of defeat in her throat, but didn't dare to try to do anything about it, as Willa tore off a piece of silver tape and covered up her name on the tag.

She seriously considered the black marker for a few seconds, but she was almost sure that Valerie would pursue some sort of harassment suit against her. Fortunately, Willa always kept something to write with in her purse at all times, because it was almost a daily occurrence for someone to want a book signed or an autograph. She used the pen to outline the letters over the tape and then color them in to create her nickname. There was no way she was going to walk around all night with Willamina written on her chest.

Silver streamers, tablecloths, balloons, and centerpieces decorated the interior of the gymnasium. If it weren't for the banner spread across the stage area with their class year printed on it, it would have looked like a celebration of someone's fiftieth birthday party. Apparently, since nothing ever happened in this town, mostly everyone had shown up right on time to the event. The entire room was swarming with people and Willa was grateful for the dimmed lighting to keep their entrance as low key as possible. She spotted an empty table in the back corner of the room, which she swiftly crossed over to, with her head bowed down, and planted herself into one of the seats.

Shannon sat down next to Willa but Megan remained standing and leaned in to give instructions to Shannon. "You stay here and defend our girl if she needs it. I'll go get drinks for us."

Shannon smiled, and it made Willa appreciate that Megan was so willing to offer her a role to play in their newly formed group. Willa looked over to her with a guilty expression after she overheard what Megan had told her. "Please don't let me hold you back from socializing. This room is probably packed with people that you know."

"The problem with being the town doctor is that I know all of the most personal aspects of everyone's lives, and yet because of that, no one wants to associate with me outside of that patient to doctor relationship. While I understand that there is a level of embarrassment that they must feel, I wish that I could convince them that I can separate work from social interactions."

"Considering that you must have almost every single person as a patient on this island, that sounds horribly lonely. In case you haven't noticed, I have a similar problem in the friend department. At least we have each other," Willa smiled as she caught sight of Megan pushing her way through the crowd on her way back to their table, "and our fearless leader makes us the perfect party of three."

"I'll toast to that."

Megan made it back after a harrowing balancing act through a packed room, carrying two armfuls, which included a mixture of bottles and cups. "I wasn't sure what everyone wanted, so I got a little bit of everything."

Willa grinned. "At least we have a professional to mix us up something tasty."

Most of the night consisted of the three women enjoying the sort of small talk involved with getting acquainted with one another. They also spent a good amount of time commenting on the attire choices that their former classmates were wearing, as well as how twenty years can really change how people looked.

Every now and then someone would wander over to their hidden table in the corner and strike up a conversation, but it seemed to increase more so as the alcohol began to hit their systems. Willa found that she could place each of them into one of three categories. First, there were the ones that just completely ignored her presence altogether when they approached the table. They would greet Megan with cheer because she provided the town with beer and food. Shannon would get a professional nod of appreciation for keeping them healthy, and Willa wouldn't get so much as a glance in her direction, which she didn't mind at all.

The second group consisted of the ones that put on a fake sense of excitement over seeing her. They pretended as though they had once shared a deep connection when they were in school and that they were devastated when they lost touch over the years. These people were the ones that pulled a chair up to Willa's and wanted to discuss every major film and book she worked on and begged for details on what it was like to meet the famous people involved with her projects. This group was annoying but Willa was used to dealing with people like that on a regular basis.

The last type, which was the most difficult to process, were the ones that outwardly chastised her for committing Brynn to a lifetime in a wheelchair. Brynn's old teammates were the most protective of her, angry that her athletic career was wasted before it really began. Girls that had crushes on Griffin spat out comments that he shouldn't have been with someone who cheated on him with his own sister right in front of him. The one that she was currently dealing with, though, was one of Griffin's friends, who wobbled very unsteadily over to stand above Willa.

"Griff gave up his entire college scholarship because his sister needed him to take care of her. Now, you have the audacity to come back here and flaunt your rich lifestyle." The tall skinny man, who Willa recognized as Ryan, reeked of vodka and sweat.

Willa began to fear that Ryan might start to express physically his anger when he began to sway aggressively from side to side. Megan thankfully recognized the signs too, because when he got a little too close to Willa, she put herself between them. "I think you should back off and find someone else to talk to."

"That bitch ruined two good people and she didn't have to do any time for her crimes." Ryan took a step closer to Megan, unwilling to back down.

This time Shannon rose from her seat. "It wouldn't look very good on the news if you were known as the drunk man who harmed the beloved Willa Barton. Take some time to sober up, and discuss your issues with her when you're capable of making logical decisions."

Ryan wasn't so bold with Shannon and slunk away slowly into the crowd of people in the center of the room. Ryan must have spread the word around that Willa had people watching out for her, because the number of unwanted visitors at their table trickled down as the night progressed.

Even though things had quieted down after he left, the adrenaline rush of the encounter agitated Megan and Shannon. Despite their continued reassurances, Willa felt guilty for keeping them from mingling with everyone else, no matter how much they tried to convince her that she wasn't. "I'm going to the ladies' room," she announced.

Megan instantly stood. "I'll go with you."

"No, please. I'll be fine. I want to wander around the halls for a bit and maybe step out for some fresh air. It's important that you both get around and socialize. I'll be gone in a week, but this town is crucial to both of your livelihoods. We can meet up at the car a little later."

Shannon placed Willa's purse in her hand and paused to make eye contact with her. Willa had become accustomed to Megan's firm but playful way of taking a role as her bodyguard, prepared to throw down and brawl if necessary. Shannon, on the other hand, seemed to genuinely take her security as a life and death matter. Willa wondered if it was because as a doctor, she must be witness to some of the horrible outcomes of people in similar situations as her. "Please don't hesitate to text us if you need help."

Willa nodded and took a deep breath as she separated from the safety net of her friends. She made her way out into the brightly lit hallway past rows of lockers until she reached the girl's bathroom. The signs in the gym had instructed the reunion guests to use the restrooms located in the gymnasium shower rooms, to help contain them to only one section of the school during the event, so she hoped that the one in the hallway would be empty. She listened as she pushed the door open slowly, but there were no sounds coming from inside, so she quickly entered before anyone caught her going in.

After struggling to get the zipper up on the back of her dress for way too long – she almost used her emergency text to Shannon – she finally got hold of the zipper. It had been so much easier to get the dress on at the house where there was plenty of room to maneuver her body, but in the tiny stall, her elbows kept hitting the metal walls.

Just as she was about to exit the constricting stall, Willa gritted her teeth as the door to the restroom opened. She stood motionless, as more than one set of footsteps entered the room. She figured that they would both enter stalls and then she could get out before they even noticed that she was there, but just the opposite happened.

Willa watched from the narrow opening in the metal door, as Cassidy, dressed in black jeans and a button up shirt with a bow tie, lifted up a woman that Willa didn't recognize, and sat her on the counter between two sinks. She watched as Cassidy leaned into the woman, kissed her neck, and nibbled at her ear. The woman moaned in delight as Cassidy pushed her hips between her thighs and pressed their lips together in a deep kiss.

A flutter of delight shot through Willa's mind when she learned that Cassidy and Brynn were not, in fact, a couple, as she had believed. She wanted Brynn to be happy but she just couldn't see her with Cassidy, especially after their altercation with each other this afternoon.

All Willa had to do was quietly wait out Cassidy's make out session with her date until she was done. She

considered facing her opposition head on by walking
out now, but she had waited so long at this point that it
would be obvious that she had been watching them the
whole time. Cassidy had already accused her of being
a stalker once that day. She decided to just take a step
back away from the door and wait patiently, but she
mistakenly let her purse swing off her shoulder, which
in turn set off the motion sensor on the automatic
toilet flushing system.

Willa winced and covered her mouth with her
fingers to suppress any sounds of regret that might
escape from it. Her mind raced as she fully expected
Cassidy to bash down the door and punish her for
intruding on their intimate moment, but nothing of
the sort happened. Instead, Cassidy hooked her arm
around the woman's waist and swept her down from
the counter. With faces red from the embarrassment
of being caught making out in a high school bathroom,
they retreated swiftly from the room, giggling as they
scurried into the hallway.

It made her a little leery of the situation to see
the way that Cassidy was so quick to hide her actions.
She hoped for Brynn's sake that they weren't actually
together, because that meant that Willa had just become
a witness to an affair. Everything was just speculation
at this point and she doubted that Brynn would listen
to anything she had to say anyway.

She slid open the latch to the door and shook her
head at herself for being afraid of such a silly situation.
Being located in their old atmosphere for the evening
gave off an illusion that things hadn't changed in
twenty years. She had to keep reminding herself that
she and everyone else in this town were no longer
teenagers. Bullying and a hierarchy of friends to back

them up over childish issues shouldn't solve problems. She would no longer run from the comments thrown at her or hide behind people willing to defend her.

She only needed to confront two people directly, and in time, she was determined to do just that. With a newfound confidence, Willa strode into the lobby of the school, only to find that it was void of any people. The walls were still painted in the maroon and light blue stripes that they had been twenty years ago and she followed them down the hall until she reached a large glass trophy case. While the names and dates on the various trophies, ribbons, and metals in the case spanned from the nineteen-seventies all the way to current times, the two names that were engraved on most of the awards on the shelves belonged to Brynn and Griffin Reed. No one in the history of Laurel Cove High could compete even close to the level of athletic ability that the Reed twins had.

As Willa peered in, slightly hunched over to get a better view on a lower shelf, recalling some of the highlights of the wins represented in the case, she just barely picked up on the sound of rubber wheels gliding along the shiny surface of the terrazzo floor. Willa pushed the purse straps that had slid down her bare shoulder back up and clung to the bulky leather bag as if it were a life preserver that could keep her afloat. When she finally built up the nerve enough to turn towards Brynn, she took a long moment to take in the sight of the dearest friend that she ever had.

Brynn had paused motionless, gripping the wheels of her chair. Willa wondered if it was because she was considering retreating in the opposite direction or if she might be preparing to gain enough momentum to collide directly into her. Either way, she wouldn't blame her decision, which she believed that she was deserving of.

Brynn was dressed in a black men's suit that was precisely tailored to fit the curves of her body perfectly. Her tie was a bright shade of cobalt blue that was an identical match to Willa's dress. If a stranger were to approach them in the hall, it would appear as though these two women had coordinated to dress together as a couple for the evening.

Willa's greatest fear for the past twenty years had been that someday she would eventually have to look Brynn in the eyes. It was something that she imagined doing a countless number of times in her mind, and yet the thought of doing it brought her to the point of breaking down. Now that the reality of the moment faced her, she could feel her heart racing with anticipation. When she lifted her eyes, the overwhelming sadness was there, but the calming sensation that Brynn had always provided her with was also there.

Brynn's irises were the deep shade of blue like the night sky that surrounds the moon. As Willa looked into them from down the hallway, she was relieved to see that there didn't appear to be anger hidden within their depths. In fact, if she was reading Brynn's expression correctly, it almost seemed as though she was looking forward to seeing her. Willa could feel the tears welling up under her eyelids so she lifted the corners of her mouth up to hide the pain and to attempt to keep the tears from falling down her cheeks.

The fake wall that Willa was putting up was evident. Brynn raised her eyebrows and looked to Willa with a questioning expression that silently asked for permission for her to come closer. Willa understood what Brynn was asking of her and she extended her arm out with her palm up to accept the invitation. Brynn pushed forward on her wheels, letting the smooth surface of the floor propel her with calculated ease towards Willa.

For a single precious moment, Willa felt as though she could handle whatever would come next between her and Brynn. She was prepared to accept any emotions that Brynn would throw at her and to allow herself to express what she was thinking and feeling without holding anything back. She knew that this was what they both needed so badly, regardless of the outcome.

All of her hopes were shattered, though, when the shadow of a figure stepped out into the hallway behind Brynn. Willa's eyes widened as she immediately saw the hulking presence of Griffin come into view behind Brynn.

Griffin was also dressed impressively, adorned in the mirror image of Brynn's suit. There was no denying the stark resemblance of the Reed twins, not only in their physical appearance but also in their mannerisms and confident personalities. With their combined dashingly good looks and charismatic charm, they were the most sought after members of their class, although neither one of them showed interest in anyone else when Willa was around.

Willa's initial reaction to seeing Griffin was one of awe for the boy that she once cared for dearly when she was young. While those feelings were lost over the years, he still held a place in her heart for the friendship that she shared with him for so long. When she looked to him for the same yielding of past conflicts as Brynn did, there was nothing but a cold and hateful disdain enveloping him.

He broke the peaceful silent exchanges between the two women by filling the space with the pounding of his footsteps across the floor, in his haste to cover as much ground as quickly as possible. He stopped just behind Brynn and arched his back over her. He made it known with his show of ownership that Brynn was off limits, no matter what her desires were. He solidified the deal further by flashing Willa a look of disapproval for even thinking about getting close to his property. The rage shown as Griffin puffed out his chest in protest of her being anywhere near his sister made her back away slowly. Brynn shook her head in objection of the distance Willa put between them and reached out to her, but she was already retreating beyond reach.

A hard, protruding object jabbed into the lower portion of Willa's back and she turned to see that it was the banister to a flight of stairs leading up to the second floor. Without hesitation, she ascended the first set of steps. Just before she rounded the corner to the second set, she glanced down to the base of the stairs. Brynn had followed her as far as her wheels would allow, hitting the barrier of the bottom step. Her hand wrapped tightly around the railing, and Willa was sure that if Brynn could have followed her on pure will alone, she would have. What broke Willa's heart was the shattered look that Brynn gave her for running away. It was cowardly for her to escape to the one place that Brynn didn't have access to, and the hurt on Brynn's face was gut wrenching.

Willa hesitated, wanting to fix the pain that she caused, but Griffin still lurked below, and along with that, the eminent threat issued by him if she dared to return.

The only place for her to go was up, and so she

continued until she was pushing the metal bar that opened the door to the second level of the school. The door slammed shut behind her and clicked into place, sending an almost deafening echo down the empty hallway. As if the memories of her teenage self led Willa, she went directly to the third door on the left and stepped into the classroom located there.

The room was simple as far as decoration goes, in comparison to the others in the building, because it was primarily used for English classes. Other than the student's desks, seats, and blackboard, there was only the teacher's desk at the front of the room. It particularly stood out though, because unlike the generic metal desk that every other teacher had, this one was a massive hardwood oak writing desk. Willa made her way over to it, and rolled out the equally impressive high backed leather chair from behind it, to take a seat.

Out of all four years spent at this school, she felt most at home here in this room. She never had to put effort, as the other students did, into the assignments given in this room. Everything having to do with reading, writing, literature, and composition came easily to her. It was no wonder, when in her time of agony as an adult, she ran here for comfort.

Walking away from Brynn was a painstakingly difficult decision, but she had not, in any way, prepared herself to confront Griffin. To take on both of them at once would have been detrimental to her psychological state. Her hand was still shaking from the mere thought of what Griffin might have to say to her. The trembling made it nearly impossible to retrieve her cell phone from her purse and type out the three digits of the room number that she was in.

Within the span of just a couple of minutes, Shannon and Megan entered the classroom, their eyes darting suspiciously at their surroundings. Willa tapped her hand over her heart. She wanted them to know that she was alone and they didn't have to worry about fending off anyone else.

If it weren't for the stark contrast of her blonde hair and the shimmering blue of her dress, it might have been difficult to see Willa huddled against the height of the black leather chair. She felt quite small compared to the immense desk and chair she was sitting at. She wished that the large pieces of furniture could just consume her. Anything would be better than having to face a single one of her other former classmates, besides the two that were currently in her presence.

Shannon was by Willa's side in a matter of a few strides, while Megan made herself look busy by checking out a textbook left on a desk on the opposite side of the classroom. Shannon took one of Willa's hands in hers while the other one wrapped around her wrist. If anyone else were doing this, it might seem as though it was a comforting gesture by a concerned friend, but Willa could tell by the slight pressure on her wrist, and the calculating look on Shannon's face, that she was checking her pulse.

"What are my chances of survival, Doc?"

Shannon released Willa's wrist and grinned. "You'll be fine, but I think you should refrain from any more stressful social interactions tonight."

Willa let out an exaggerated sigh. "Ha, you don't have to do much to convince me of that."

When Shannon appeared satisfied that Willa wasn't on the verge of a panic attack, she backed away from the desk that she had been leaning against. "I guess we know what Laurel Cove is spending our tax money on, don't we?" She ran her fingers over the intricate designs carved into the wood.

A shy look swept over Willa's face; she didn't want anyone to know, but she couldn't allow the school budget to be blamed. "Actually, I had the desk and chair delivered to the school as a gift. Without the teachers in the English department, I doubt that I would have ever narrowed down my academic interests to creative writing. I often wonder where I might have ended up if it weren't for the stories that I first began to create in this very room."

"I would say this was a pretty nice way to say thank you," Megan said, finally joining in on the conversation now that it had shifted from health to talking about the school.

"It's a great idea, actually. I should do something to show my appreciation to the science department," Shannon added.

"I don't suppose the detention hall needs sprucing up," Megan teasingly mentioned.

Willa smirked at Megan's remark, but then returned to Shannon's comment. "Do you honestly think you would have chosen to enter any field other than medical, with your father being who he is?"

"I considered other options, and I'd like to believe that he would have supported me no matter what, but in the end, I felt a calling to help people as much as he did."

Willa's face softened at the memory of Shannon helping her. "I always wanted to thank you for being there for me the night of the graduation party."

"While my father was busy attending to Brynn

until they could airlift her off the island, I just did what I could to stop the bleeding to your head. It's still a mystery what caused the injury to your head, isn't it?"

"Yes; all I remember is waking up and you were holding a cold towel to my head."

"It was a bad concussion. You were unconscious for a little while. Everyone was concerned about Brynn, but you had a serious injury too."

Willa was quiet for a moment while she absorbed Shannon's recollection of that night. "There were quite a few times when I wished I hadn't woken up," she said in a voice so soft, it was barely a whisper.

Megan and Shannon locked eyes in a frantic exchange. It was something that Willa had never shared before, not even in therapy sessions.

Megan made her way around the desk and situated herself onto one corner of the chair, balancing an arm around Willa's neck to keep from sliding off. She planted a light kiss on Willa's forehead. "Oh, sweetie, your daddy's heart would have broken long before it did, if anything had happened to you back then."

"I don't even have *him* anymore."

"You have us now." Megan held her hand out to Shannon to join them even closer than she already was. Shannon took Megan's hand and rested her other one on Willa's shoulder. "We can be your Laurel Cove family," Megan vowed.

"Yes, please don't hesitate to call us if you feel that way ever again." Shannon's proclamation of support came across as sounding a tad more like an official medical statement, but Willa sympathized with the fact that friendships were a new concept to Shannon as well.

"I promise I will." Willa let the corners of her mouth turn up into a slight smile despite the turmoil swelling in her chest. She had allowed too many years to pass without letting people into her private life. If there could possibly be a chance for her to open herself up to that again, these two women surrounding her in a circle of protection would be the ones that she would choose. For the time being, though, she just wanted the hectic night to be over with. "Can we get out of here now? This place smells atrocious."

Chapter Nine

Willa woke up early enough to drive to the mainland to pick up an array of fresh vegetables from the farmer's market. Her contribution to the barbecue at Shannon's house was going to be a salad and vegetable skewers, but she also couldn't help but to pick up a bouquet of daisies and a couple of bottles of wine for some added fun to the evening.

It was still quite early by the time she got back to the island, so she decided to get in a run before the afternoon sun got too intense. She slipped into a pair of skintight jogging pants as well as a tank top and stepped out into the driveway. She did a few easy stretches, feeling the tenderness in her ankles from wearing high heels the previous night. After a slight adjustment to her earbuds and choosing the right song to accompany the level of energy that she wanted to attain on her jog, she took off down the road.

Her head rose instinctively to inhale the fresh, salty air that blew in directly off the ocean. In New York, she was so used to putting the miles in every day on a treadmill, just to avoid the smog of the city from entering into her system. Multiple song changes later, she found herself venturing down obscure roads that she didn't recall ever going down before. Many of the smaller ones, the farther out she went, were lacking sidewalks and she was forced to run on the gravel that lined the edges of the pavement. On one particularly sharp intersection, Willa turned the corner and the next thing she knew, she was knocked off her feet. Her arms flung out wildly to grasp at anything to keep herself from falling, but the inevitable thud as her body hit the ground occurred when nothing was available in reach.

A combination of things led to the accident, including taking the turn too fast, the blinding sun concealing her vision, and the headphones blocking out any possible warning sounds. Before she could realize what was happening, Willa found herself rolling down into the ditch on the side of the road, in a fury of gravel spraying up into the air around her. She waved a hand in front of her face and swiped at the settling particles of dirt that clung to the layer of sweat coating her body. The gritty feeling in her mouth when she licked her lips made her sit up and spit out what she could from between her teeth.

A panicked voice from above her yelled out. "Shit! Willa, are you okay?"

Willa pushed aside the strands that had come loose from her hair tie, so that she could focus on the source of the voice. Someone on an odd-looking three-wheeled bicycle was leaning over the edge of it and trying to reach out to her. Willa looked from the rider to the bike, and tried to shake the confusion from her mind as she rubbed at her forehead with the palm of her hand. How could she have collided with such a strange contraption and feel as though a bus hit her?

It wasn't until the rider pulled off her helmet and sunglasses that Willa found herself staring up at Brynn. She didn't know what to say in the moment, sitting on the side of the road, covered in dirt and feeling at her lowest, so she started rambling. "I'm so sorry. I didn't see you right in front of me. I shouldn't have had my music on so loud. It was stupid of me really. Did I hurt you?"

"Willa, I'm fine." Brynn motioned to her custom-made bike. "This thing is built with sturdy metal – it's made to withstand heavy-duty trail riding – so it probably did much more damage to you than the impact I took. Can you stand?"

Willa pushed up off the ground with one hand and slowly stood up. She brushed more gravel off herself and nodded to Brynn that everything seemed to be in working order. She was still a few feet below street level in the ditch, though, so she took a step forward to climb out of it. It was at that point, when she tried to put weight on one leg, that a searing pain shot up from her right knee. Willa yelped out in pain and had to readjust her weight off that leg to stay in an upright position. She bent down to search the area of her leg where the pain was coming from, and found a hole torn into the fabric of her jogging pants. The area surrounding the hole was wet and slowly increasing in size with added moisture. Subconsciously, Willa already knew what it was, but she couldn't help but place her fingertips on the saturated material. When she pulled them away, they shimmered with a bright crimson liquid in the sunlight.

The sight of blood smeared on her fingers made Willa's head spin. The only thing that grounded her back from nearly passing out was the sound of Brynn's voice. "Take my hand," Brynn instructed. Willa fought through her spinning vision to see Brynn reaching out to her as far as she could over the side of her bike.

Willa shook herself out of her trance and tried to make getting up to the road her focal point, even if internally she was freaking out. She grasped onto Brynn's hand for support, but gave her a questioning look, not wanting to pull her down with her. Brynn reassured her by tapping at the strap around her waist, which kept her tied securely onto the seat of the bike. Willa pushed through the pain and half climbed, but mostly let the power in Brynn's arm drag her up.

When she finally reached the solid ground of the pavement again, Willa tried to examine the site of the injury, but she winced every time she came close to touching it and flailed her hands up in dismay. When she looked up, she caught Brynn watching her every move with an amused grin on her face. "Why is this so funny to you?"

"You were always afraid of the tiniest bit of blood. Remember that time you passed out when I got a bloody nose playing basketball?"

Willa put a hand up to stop Brynn from talking. "Ugh, don't remind me of that right now."

"Sorry." Brynn released the strap around her waist so that she could sit up straighter, and patted the soft pad of her bike where her chest rested when she pedaled with her hands. "Come sit here so we can check out your injury."

She limped over to the bike but paused when she got close to where Brynn wanted her to sit. It was one thing for her to be thrust into an unexpected encounter with Brynn due to an accident, but to purposefully sit within inches of her so early on in their juncture intimidated her. Brynn must have picked up on Willa's apprehension, because she guided her along with a gentle hand on her forearm and a convincing smile. Willa figured that if Brynn had any ill intent towards her, she could have easily left her behind in the ditch.

She balanced her bottom onto the cushioned pad and stretched her good leg up and onto one of the metal bars along the side of Brynn's seat for support. Brynn reached down and slowly raised Willa's hurt leg with easy movements, careful not to bend her knee too far, until her foot was planted directly in Brynn's lap.

Brynn pulled her thin biking gloves off, and shoved them into a small pouch attached to her seat. She then went to work at trying to lift the bottom of Willa's jogging pants up, but they were skintight and wouldn't roll up past her ankle. She transferred her focus up to where the wound was located, but the hole didn't offer enough space to get a good look at what they were dealing with. Brynn gingerly stuck one finger from each hand into the opening and pulled the fabric up and away from Willa's skin.

A devious look swept over Brynn's face as she held Willa's gaze in hers. "You don't have any special attachment to this particular pair of pants, do you?"

"No, they're already ruined anyway. Why?"

"Because I'm about to tear them off of you."

Willa narrowed her eyes until she was playfully glaring at Brynn. "Oh, just do it." She waved an approving hand towards her knee. "I'm sure you've been fantasizing about this for years."

Brynn shrugged her shoulders, not revealing whether she cared either way, yet the slight blush creeping up in her cheeks gave away her true feelings about it. With a quick, strong tug, she ripped from the knee all the way down to the cuff of the pants. The open flap allowed her to fold the excess fabric up under Willa's thigh. With the entire lower half of Willa's leg exposed, Brynn was able to get a view of the wound. Due to the angle that Willa was sitting, though, she couldn't see a thing, but the way that Brynn was scrunching up her face didn't give her a positive inclination about it. Willa leaned over so that she could check out the injury herself.

A firm palm to her chest prevented Willa from going as far as she could, but Brynn was just a little too late, because Willa had gotten close enough to catch sight of how much blood was running down her leg. Her face paled over and she swayed significantly from side to side. It was a tossup which sensation was worse: the images of bright stars flashing across her vision, or the bile that was beginning to rise up in her throat.

Brynn kept her hand on Willa's chest and tried to steady her because she was dangerously close to falling off the tiny platform that she was balancing on. "Close your eyes and take deep breaths."

Willa did as she was told, and opened her eyes when the risk of her passing out or vomiting had gone by. The comforting eyes of Brynn met her, who knew just how intolerant of the sight of blood she was. "I'm good now," she tried to reassure Brynn.

Brynn observed Willa with her sweat covered brow and gasping breaths. "Sure you are." Brynn reached for her water bottle and handed it over to Willa, knowing that she needed to hydrate.

Willa let out a grin at Brynn's teasing remark and then motioned down at her knee, afraid to even glance in that direction. "Can you cover it up so that I can make it back home?"

Brynn nodded and took the water bottle back from Willa's hand. She felt a gentle stream of water being squirted on the surrounding area, but not directly onto the actual site of the cut. Tiny rivers of water, blood, and dirt flowed down Willa's calf and soaked up into her sock. She did her best to hold back the gagging reflex at the base of her throat. Then Brynn handed the water bottle back to her. "Drink more," Brynn insisted.

Willa tipped the bottle back and swallowed down quite a few large gulps of water. It was just as she lowered her head back down, when a shot of pain ripped through her leg. "Ah, fuck," she yelled out.

When the wave of intense agony passed, she was able to assess what had taken place while she was busy hydrating. Brynn's T-shirt was off, which left her wearing only a sports bra. The missing shirt was now wrapped tightly around her knee and absorbing the blood that had been gushing out of the wound. Willa realized that Brynn had distracted her with the water just long enough to fix her up with the only thing she had available.

Brynn waved her hand back and forth in front of Willa's face. "It's safe for you to look now. The gash is covered up as well as most of the blood."

She snapped back in a state of embarrassment when she became conscious of the fact that she had been absentmindedly staring at the perfectly shaped abs on Brynn's stomach. "Uh, thanks for your help," she said as she started to pull her leg out of Brynn's lap.

"You're not going anywhere," Brynn insisted, holding her foot firmly in place.

Before she could protest, Brynn was removing Willa's cell phone out of the armband holder around her bicep. She tugged the headphones out of the audio port and dropped the tangled mess into Willa's lap. As a rule, Willa would never let anyone have access to her phone and most certainly not search through it, but she watched now in silent fascination as Brynn chose one of her contacts and made a call.

"Hey, it's Brynn. Can you come to the corner of Forest and Shore Road? Willa's going to need stitches." Brynn listened while the person on the other line spoke. "Thanks, we'll see you in a few minutes."

When Brynn returned her phone, she looked down at the screen and saw that she called Shannon. "I could have gone to the clinic."

"It's Sunday; the clinic is closed and you can hardly stand, let alone walk there or home, for that matter. Shannon won't mind coming to get you. I heard that she stuck close by your side last night."

"She wouldn't have needed to if your friends hadn't been verbally attacking me all evening."

Brynn raised her hand up in defense. "Whoa, I had no idea they were being rude to you. I reamed out Cass already for what she said to you at the gym." Brynn tapped the side of Willa's good leg. "Speaking of the gym, you should be using the treadmills there instead of risking your life on these narrow roads."

"Probably, but I'd rather take my chances with the ditch, than have to deal with Griffin."

"If you stop by after three o'clock he'll be gone. That is, if you don't mind having to deal with me?"

"Maybe I'll stop by if I have time tomorrow..." Willa drifted off, not wanting to commit to something that she would regret later.

Brynn's fingers wrapped around Willa's hand. "Your dad had a membership to the gym, he had a locker there, and you should be the one to come empty out his possessions from it."

While she was grateful that Brynn hadn't brought up anything regarding the accident twenty years ago, to talk about her father with the one other person who cared about him as much as she did was just as difficult of a conversation to have. She was well aware that her father had maintained a close relationship with Brynn over the years, but he kept any information about it to himself, because she had asked him not to interfere with trying to mend any fences between the two of them. Willa had been absolutely sure that Brynn never wanted to see her again, so she assumed that it was pointless to put her father in between them. A huge reason why Griffin, Brynn, and Willa had become such great friends as children was because Willa didn't have a mother and the twins didn't have a father. When they all came together, there weren't as many missing parts to their families.

Willa closed her eyes, not wanting to fall apart on the side of the road without the option of being able to walk away if she wanted to. Brynn respected her silence and held her hand until Shannon pulled up in her vehicle and lent her support to get Willa on her feet.

The instant Willa's hand separated from Brynn's, she missed the touch of Brynn's fingers covering hers. It caused her to flash back to the moment when she last saw Brynn laying on the concrete, soaking wet, and reaching for Willa's hand. She had tried, even with a bloody head injury, to inch her way to Brynn's side, but Griffin had blocked her from getting any closer.

The same feeling resurfaced now as Shannon whisked her away to the SUV and buckled her into the seat. As they pulled away from the side of the road, Willa pressed her forehead against the window and mouthed the words, "thank you," to Brynn.

Chapter Ten

That was quite possibly the most embarrassing thing that could ever happen to me," Willa groaned from the Adirondack chair as she looked toward the ocean from Shannon's patio. "I mean, seriously, I rammed right into her."

Megan swatted at the smoke billowing up from the grill and then poked a temperature gage into the center of one of the thick steaks that she had flipped. "I think some people would call that fate, my dear."

"If that's fate, then whoever is running my life has a very twisted sense of humor. It's fortunate that she didn't get hurt in *this* accident. I'm pretty sure that if she did, Laurel Cove would kick me out and condemn me as an official endangerment to the town."

Megan tried to suppress a grin. "It did bring you two together again, even if the chance meeting wasn't a graceful one by any means."

Willa folded her arms across her chest in protest. "There are a million other ways that I would have preferred to *that* particular instance, though."

"The real question is, would you have had the nerve enough to approach her on your own before your time on the island was up?"

"Ugh, you're right. I wouldn't have, but allow me to sulk about it for a little while, will you?" Willa stuck out her bottom lip and glared at the beautiful view.

"I grant you permission to be as grumpy as you

want now, but as soon as we finish off this bottle of wine, there had better be a smile on that face of yours." Megan refilled Willa's glass and gave her a wink before taking her place next to the grill again. "You wanted your steak well done, right?"

"Yes, please, I've seen enough blood for one day."

The screen door slid open and Shannon emerged from inside the house. "Speaking of blood, you need to start following the doctor's orders and get that leg raised." Shannon lifted Willa's leg up and pushed a hassock with a pillow under it, before setting it back down.

Willa opened her mouth to spit out a witty comment about how there should be lines drawn between doctor time and friend time, but before she could, an ice pack was planted firmly on her knee over the thick layer of gauze covering the stitches. "Thanks for coming to my rescue, again."

"You're welcome, but you should be thanking Brynn for the last one. Without her, I highly doubt you would have called me to help you."

Willa turned her face to hide a sheepish look.

"So, you've caught on to her stubborn streak already, huh?" Megan chimed in from across the patio.

Shannon passed by Megan and patted her shoulder in agreement, carrying an armful of plates and silverware. "She's just used to being independent, but eventually she'll catch on to the idea of relying on her friends when she needs us," she said, purposefully loud enough for Willa to hear.

"I can hear you talking about me, but you're both right, and I'm willing to toast to that." Willa raised her glass above her head. Shannon and Megan followed her lead and they all finished off the wine in their glasses.

"It's time to pop open a new bottle, because dinner is served, ladies," Shannon announced.

Willa rose from her seat, holding her leg as still as possible. She was lucky that the cut was just below her knee so that she wouldn't tear the stitches every time she bent it. Shannon had threatened her with the prospect of crutches if that had been the case, and that was enough to scare her into taking it easy for a while, until it had time to heal properly.

The conversation started light during dinner, but the three women took the opportunity to get to know one another better. "Do you think you'll have any more children there, mamma bear?" Willa asked Megan.

Megan finished chewing a bite of salad. "One was plenty. I'm definitely done, but I wouldn't trade her for anything. She's the one accomplishment that I'm most proud of in my life."

Willa plopped another skewer onto Shannon's plate to replace the empty stick that she had just tossed into the trash. "What about you, any plans for a family?"

"I'm too busy taking care of everyone else to have kids of my own, but I wouldn't mind settling down with someone if the right man came along."

"Those are impossible to find." Megan shook her head in disgust. "Any babies on the horizon for Ms. Barton?"

Willa crinkled up her nose. "Babies and writing are never a good combination. My fellow authors who tried it don't recommend it."

"What if you're with someone who does the child rearing while you focus on your career?" Shannon inquired.

"As progressive as our society claims to be, most men don't want to play housewife while their spouse is off earning a living."

"True, but as far as I can tell, you tend to only date women," Megan commented with a sly grin.

The statement that Megan posed was not something that Willa was prepared to discuss. She had always known heading into press interviews what might come up and how to respond to the more personal questions. Mostly she could get away with a vague reply, or better yet, to divert the question in a different direction, but these were her new friends and they deserved a more honest answer. "It's true; all of my relationships after Griffin have been with females. To be honest, I should have been with Brynn back then and not Griff, but I can't change the past. All of my current relationships have thus far been short lived, to say the least. I've definitely not found *Ms. Right* yet."

"So, it wasn't a rumor; you did date that director from your latest movie?" Megan asked.

"Yes, she and I were together for a little while, but her work kept her mostly on the west coast and with me being based in New York, the distance separated us too often."

"But you're not openly out to the public, are you? I mean, the media played it out to be a big Hollywood secret."

"No, and it's really just because of what happened here that's keeping me in the closet. I either look like a straight woman who was angry at her lesbian friend and caused her to become a paraplegic, or I'm the closeted lesbian who cheated on her boyfriend with his sister, or I am a bisexual who went after her twin best friends and ruined both of their lives. No matter how you look at it, I come off to the people who know my history as a horrible person." Willa pushed around a tomato in her salad bowl. "I long for the day when I can come out to my fans as a proud lesbian, though."

Shannon worked at cutting a slice of steak with the precision of a doctor. "Hopefully you can work towards resolving some of those misconceptions while you're in Laurel Cove so that things will be easier for you when you go back home."

"It would be a miracle if I could accomplish all that, but what really matters is if I can find a way to apologize to Brynn."

"How did she react to seeing you this afternoon? Did she give you any indication that she didn't want to see you again?" Megan asked.

"No, just the opposite, actually. She invited me to the gym to get some of my father's possessions from his locker."

"Well, that's a good thing, right?"

"I suppose, but she was almost too nice. Our conversation fell into place, like when we were teenagers."

"Brynn has had twenty years to come to terms with her injuries. Often times guilt is more difficult to let go of than blame," Shannon added with an empathetic tone.

"Thank you for your kind advice. You've filled in nicely in the absence of the psychologist that I should be seeing."

Shannon gave Willa a look of a child that has done something wrong, but then promptly softened into the expression of a compassionate friend. "I've had to take my fair share of psych classes in college."

After dinner, Megan insisted on taking over the

job of cleaning up on her own, because Shannon had offered up her house for their gathering and she treated Willa as if she had just undergone major surgery. Willa gave in after Shannon tossed another fresh ice pack at her, along with a very stern look.

While Megan disappeared into the house to wash dishes, Shannon sat on one side of a long wooden porch swing and Willa took a spot on the other side. She extended her injured leg out over the armrest to keep it elevated and avoid potential nagging from her doctor friend. They glided back and forth and Willa reached down to her waist to loosen the string on her linen pants. She wished that she had packed more pairs of the free-flowing pants in her luggage, as she now pulled the fabric gingerly away from the site of her wound. She didn't have many other clothing options to choose from during her healing process.

They both appreciated the peaceful atmosphere of the summer sounds of the coast for a considerable amount of time. Willa had almost forgotten that she wasn't alone as her eyes wandered deep in solace up at the clouds, until Shannon voiced her concern. "Are you worrying about how tomorrow will go with Brynn?"

Willa blinked out of her daze and tilted her head so that she could give her attention to Shannon. "Some, but if I were to accidentally run into Griffin, I was also trying to figure out how to apologize for holding him back from college."

Shannon sucked in a deep breath and puffed out her cheeks as she slowly released it. "You're referring to the rumor that you, along with everyone else in this town, believe that Griffin stayed behind to help take care of his sister."

Willa narrowed her eyes and turned so that she

was close enough to whisper in Shannon's ear. "What do you mean by *rumor*?"

Shannon's brow furrowed and her head ever so slightly shifted from side to side. "He's technically a patient at the clinic, Willa; I can't divulge confidential information. The important thing is that you know that *you* are not to blame for him not going to college." With that, she left the swing and Willa swaying in it at an awkward angle with legs splayed in two different directions.

The concentrated area of pain below her knee began to dissipate as the new information about her past left her feeling as if she had walked face first into a cement pillar. So many thoughts and questions rushed through her mind that it didn't even register to her that someone was calling out her name. She nearly jumped out of her own skin when Megan's face appeared in her line of vision.

"Oh, sweetie, we need to hurry through dessert so that you can go get some much-needed rest." Megan held out her arm to help Willa to her feet. "Maybe Doctor Martin can hook you up with something to help knock you out, if you know what I mean." Megan winked after, and looked to make sure that Shannon hadn't overheard her comment.

Shannon placed a pie with perfectly golden crust and little wisps of steam escaping from the holes in the top of it in the center of the table. Megan rubbed her palms together and licked her lips.

"The Anchor makes some of the best pies in town. What are you so excited about?" Shannon asked.

"It's true what they say, food always tastes better when somebody else cooks it."

Shannon lifted a slice out and placed it in front

of Megan first, because she was already picking off the edges of crust that curved over the sides of the dish. Megan's eyes widened at the sight of the plump berries and thick red juice that flowed out of the perfectly cut triangle. "No way! Are these strawberries from Mr. Carter's garden?" She was bouncing on the edge of her seat like a child ready for recess.

Shannon let out a mischievous grin but didn't answer Megan.

"Is old man Carter still alive? That guy was ancient back when we were kids," Willa wondered, not having seen him yet since she had returned to the Cove. "All I remember is that he yelled when anyone went near his garden but he was too slow to chase us off because of the bunions on his feet."

"I may have made a trade for free medical care in exchange for some berries."

The fork on its way to Megan's mouth stopped in mid motion and hovered just below her lips. Her face swept over in a yellowish green tint and the corners of her mouth turned down. Shannon and Willa looked at one another with bites of pie in their mouths. They both knew that it tasted as delicious as it looked so they couldn't figure out what her problem was.

"Please tell me you washed your hands before picking the berries, after touching his nasty feet."

The three women erupted into a round of laughter that continued long until the sun dipped down, so low that the chill of the air had them rubbing their arms for warmth.

Chapter Eleven

Typically, the first priority in Willa's life was to focus on her current writing project, whether it was a novel or movie script. Very few other aspects of her life came first over the fictional lives of her characters. Ever since her arrival in Laurel Cove, though, her creativity was taking a backseat to everything else happening on the island.

Willa stood in the center of her father's living room and, as she spun in a circle, trying to decide on what she should do next, she concluded that she hadn't really accomplished anything at all as far as preparing the house to be sold. The cardboard box that she had placed on the coffee table was still empty after debating what to pack in it for over an hour. For some reason, the objects only seemed at place here in this home. In any other environment, she feared that they would lose the sense of purpose that her father had given them. In a box, they would become nothing more than a distant memory.

After another unsuccessful thirty minutes, she threw her hands up in the air and drove to the mainland to shop for some new outfits that accommodated her stitches. A little boutique offered some summer dresses that she purchased, but not so much in the way of pants. She figured that a sporting goods store was a good place to get some loose fitting sweat pants, which she wouldn't dare be caught wearing while in the city, but she knew that no one would give a second look at her on the island.

When the ship's wheel clock that she had taken down and then promptly placed back on the wall showed that it was almost three o'clock, Willa decided that it was time to drive to Mussels by The Sea. She hadn't officially agreed to meet Brynn, but she couldn't bear the thought of Brynn waiting for her and the disappointment that she might have when she didn't show up. Besides, emptying out her father's locker would be one tiny step in the direction of being able to complete bigger tasks ahead of her.

The gym had been newly renovated inside and had been completely modernized compared to what it was like when Willa had last been there. The floors were composed of a hard rubber substance, which dipped in slightly with every step she took. The main section that she entered into was comprised of a large room packed with various exercise equipment. A few random people were scattered around the room, going through the motions of their workout routines, but Brynn was nowhere to be seen, so Willa wandered around, trying to look like she belonged there.

She stood below one of the elaborate machines and pulled down on a handle that was attached by a cable to a stack of weights. When they didn't budge at all, she used her other hand to pull on the second handle. Her face scrunched up and she grunted while putting most of her body weight into moving the metal blocks that they were attached to. A strained smile broke out on her lips as two blocks separated from the rest, leaving a thin space just wide enough for a little light to shine between them.

"Easy there, tiger, you don't want to hurt

yourself."

With a loud clang of metal on metal, the cables that the handles were attached to flung wildly in the air when they slid out of her grip. Willa held her hands up to block any potential whacks to the head that she might get from the handles, until they settled back into place.

A hearty chuckle bellowed out as Brynn watched from a few feet away, her arms crossed under her chest and a grin spread across her face. Willa glared back at her with a scowl, as Brynn scanned the length of her body up and down, not attempting to disguise the fact that she was doing so. "I can tell that you probably have a membership to some elite fitness center in New York." Brynn paused and placed a finger to her lips while she analyzed the situation. "I would put money down that you go religiously every single day, but that you've never tried any equipment other than the treadmill and possibly the elliptical, if there aren't too many other people around to make you embarrassed to use it."

Willa dropped her hands to her hips. "Hey, maybe I don't have gigantic muscles bulging out of my arms like you do, but I'd say that I'm pretty well toned."

"I never said that you aren't. I can guarantee you watch yoga videos at home, do some squats, and most likely have a pair of five-pound dumbbells that you keep under your bed. What I'm saying is that it might be beneficial for you to have a personal trainer give you some lessons on how to use the machine that just scared the crap out of you, and maybe make the most out of your gym membership."

"Let me guess, you read that article written by a

crazy fan who stalked me for an entire day, and released every aspect of my personal life in his blog. It was filled with private details of my day, including my workout habits and even the color of my underwear."

"I'm not into reading internet gossip, although the part about your underwear might make it worth my time, but I can read a person's body type and tell what their workout routine consists of."

Willa reached up and grasped onto one of the handles of the weight machine. "So, there are other people besides me that don't know how to use one of these devices?"

"With a little personal training and lowering the amount of weight on it, you'd be fine. I could show you how everything works before you head back to the city, that way you don't have to ask someone there for help."

"Maybe I'll take you up on that offer," Willa said, once again not daring to make a solid plan. She glanced around the entire room, with a perplexed expression. "I can't picture Dad using anything in here. If he wasn't hauling traps, it wasn't worth his effort. Why would he have a membership?"

"I think you'll find your answer in his locker."

Brynn made a quick motion, which spun one wheel until she was facing the other direction. She then pointed her chin towards a row of lockers on the far wall of the room.

Willa swung her injured leg forward, using the weight of it to propel herself forward with enough speed to keep up with Brynn, who was practically flying across the floor. More often than not, she used only the rear two wheels on her chair in a seemingly perpetual wheelie.

When she finally stopped to lean against the cool

metal of the brightly colored lockers, Willa was biting down hard on her lower lip. She felt the gentle caress of a finger lightly rubbing through her cotton sweatpants, and the gauze pad covering the stitches on her leg. When she looked down, Brynn's bright blue eyes, wide with worry, met her own.

"You shouldn't be moving around so fast with fresh stitches in; they could tear."

She squeezed her eyes shut and sucked in a breath through her teeth. "I keep forgetting that."

"Do you want to sit for a while first? There's a bench over there." Brynn pointed to a waiting area near the water fountain.

"No, no, I'm fine. Which locker was his?"

"Seventy-eight." Brynn held out a tiny piece of paper with three sets of numbers scrawled on it. "Here's the code to his combination lock."

The tiny dials clicked into place as Willa spun them with the tip of her perfectly manicured thumb. When she entered the sixth and final number, she paused, and one hand came up to cover her lips so that the tiny gasp that she released was barely audible. "It's our three birthdays."

"I realized that myself a little while ago when I copied the numbers from our log book. Those were the digits that Dad—I mean, Henry picked out the day I gave him the lock, but I didn't pick up on the significance of his choice at the time."

"It's okay for you to call him that. It's been so long now that I don't remember a time when he wasn't a father figure to you. He thought of both you and Griff as his children. It should be evident how much he cared for you by this." Willa handed the paper back to Brynn.

"Thanks, I wasn't sure how you'd feel about it. Mom feels the same way about you too, you know? She'd be here now if she had the funds to get a flight back to Maine."

"Tell her not to worry about it. I have so many other burnt bridges that I have to mend while I'm here, that I think seeing your mom again might be too much for me to handle."

"Ha, yeah, although, she could help put Griff in his place."

"She's the only one that ever could," Willa agreed.

"I seem to remember you having the same ability to make him listen to reason."

"If I did at one time, I definitely don't any longer." Willa's voice faded out with an insecure sadness.

"Hey, he'll come around eventually."

Willa nodded and turned her attention back to her task. The lock slid out with a little tug and she pushed up on the small metal lever that caused the door to fling open.

One might expect to find lots of things in a gym locker. The usual items consisted of sneakers, workout clothing, and a towel. Beyond that, some people keep gear like tennis rackets, swimsuits, or a basketball. Willa wasn't sure what she was going to come across, but what was actually in there didn't have purpose in this environment, and left her genuinely confused.

Two objects sat on the bottom of the locker. There was a coffee mug handmade out of fine pottery, with a lobster painted on the side of it. It was definitely something that her father would have loved, but not anything that he would ever think to purchase for himself. Willa eyed it strangely as she pulled it out of the locker.

"It was a birthday gift from Griff a few years back," Brynn explained.

Willa nodded. That made more sense.

Below the mug was a hardcover book. Willa recognized, without removing it from its place on the bottom of the locker, what book it was. She had spent weeks working with artists, photographers, and graphic designers to come up with the perfect cover for her latest novel. Early on in her career, that was something that she had left up to her publishing company to create, but in recent years, it became a process that she enjoyed taking part in. To see her book as one of two cherished items, important enough to be locked away in safety, left her feeling melancholy.

She removed it carefully. This copy would be the last book that she had the honor of signing and sending out to her father. Immortalized on the title page were the words of gratitude that she meticulously chose and wrote out with a special fountain pen that he had given to her as a graduation present. That alone made it so much more valuable than any other book she would ever own. She faced Brynn, holding the book in one hand, the mug in the other, and raised her eyebrows in question.

"Are you ready?"

"For what?"

"I'm sure that you're curious about what those are for, so I'm going to take you out on the daily routine that Dad and I used to share together."

"I don't want to intrude on something personal that you shared. Maybe you'd rather keep it as a memory between the two of you." The truth was that Willa did want to know. She yearned to hear the stories of the years that she missed out on with her father. What she needed to know was that he lived out a fulfilling life with the people that he cared about in her absence. The only problem was that she didn't think she was prepared to learn about those things right at this very moment.

"I think I need to share this for me, just as much as Dad would have wanted you to see it for yourself."

"For *you* then…" Willa trailed off, agreeing reluctantly.

"We have a little walk ahead of us, but we can go slow, and tell me if you need to give your leg a break, okay?"

"I will."

"Good, because Shannon's a nice person, but I think she wouldn't be too happy if I called her to come to our rescue two days in a row."

Willa smiled at Brynn's joke, but she knew deep down that Shannon wouldn't mind in the least to help her again. She tucked the book under one arm and wrapped her fingers around the handle of the mug as she followed along Brynn's side, careful to stay out of the path of her wheels.

The parking lot of the gym extended out to the rear of the building, and a marked trail allowed members access to a private beach area where they could use kayaks or other rented water sports equipment from the gym. Willa assumed that they were headed in this direction, but instead, Brynn veered off to a different trail that was new to Willa. A tiny sign was posted at the entrance of the trail that read: Private Property, No Trespassing. Unlike the original trail that had a dirt surface, this one was constructed of boards.

When Brynn started to make her way down the path, Willa realized that without the boards, any sort of rain would make the ground otherwise impossible for her to use the trail in her wheelchair.

The distance to the base of the hill wasn't very far, but due to the gradual decline that was needed to make it possible for a wheelchair to be able to get back up the ramp again, the path was made in a long, zigzag pattern that took a while to navigate. The width of the path wasn't wide enough for her to walk next to Brynn, so Willa let her lead the way. She was reminded of the day she saw her at the clinic, and how fast she flew down the ramp. Brynn was very different now, moving slowly and pausing often to glance back at Willa.

Brynn had always been the strong one, the protector. Even in this moment, Willa could sense the power that she had, breaking out of the bounds that she was now restricted to, and yet still watching over her shoulder, keeping an eye on her slightly awkward friend.

At the base of the hill, where the tree line ended and the lush shades of the forest were replaced by the turquoise hues of the ocean, was a small clearing that sat high enough above sea level that the water wouldn't reach it, even during high tide. Flat cement paving stones covered the ground in the entire area, creating a smooth surface, making it easy for wheels to roll on. The thin gaps between them allowed for drainage to the earth below when it rained.

There were only two things in the clearing. One was a wooden picnic table and the other was a small shed. Willa made her way over to the table, set the mug and the book down, and ran her fingers over the smoothly varnished surface.

"Each and every one is unique and yet it's impossible not to be able to spot the craftsmanship behind a Henry Barton table. I doubt there's a backyard in the Cove without one in it," Brynn commented proudly about his work.

Willa liked the idea of a lasting legacy scattered about the island as a tribute to her father. This table was different compared to the others, though. One quarter of the table space on one side did not have a bench seat attached to it, and the leg underneath that section was curved so that there was plenty of space below it. Brynn took her place there, pulling into it and patting the seat next to her. When Willa came around to sit there, it was a little more worn down compared to the rest of the seat and there was a permanent ring stained into the surface where the coffee mug belonged.

"He built all of this, the ramp, the table, and the shed. He used a dolly to carry down the paving stones a few at a time for half a summer. This was our place; not even Griff comes down here."

"It's beautiful and secluded, but what's the purpose? I mean, there are so many other much more accessible spots on the Cove just like this. Why put so much work into this?"

"It started out as what Dad called our *lost* project. The way he explained it, he had lost you to the city and I had lost everything I knew about myself. By working on creating this, we both knew that we were held accountable to each other to show up to work on it every single day, no matter how difficult things got."

Willa swallowed with difficulty. The guilt of two people needing an escape because of her weighed heavily in her throat. "And what about after the project was finished?"

"Ah, that's where the mug and the book come into play." Brynn reached for the backpack slung over the back of her seat, then pulled out a second mug and a thermos. She filled Willa's mug as well as her own with steaming coffee. "So, every time you have a new book release, we bring it down here and read a few pages together each day until it's finished."

Willa picked up her cup, tipped it towards her lips, and blew softly on the surface before taking a long, slow sip. She set the mug back down, turning it so that the lobster was facing her and then burst out in a fit of laughter.

Brynn watched, stunned, as Willa's shoulders bounced up and down and she clutched at her stomach, unable to contain the roaring laughter from slipping out of her. When Willa noticed Brynn's somber look, she calmed herself down and placed a reassuring hand on her shoulder. "I'm sorry if I come across seeming callous about your heartfelt story. You see, all I can think of is that my lobsterman father and my athletic best friend, neither of whom ever picked up a book for pleasure a day in their lives, actually got together to read every single day."

Brynn glared back at Willa. Her cheeks twitched as she struggled to keep a straight face, but soon gave in, as a smirk spread over her lips. "It's ridiculous, I know. We had to buy a dictionary to bring with us for the first few years, until we learned some of the weird ass words you insist on using to describe things."

Willa slapped her hand on the table and again broke out into a chuckle, but this time Brynn joined in with her. "Please tell me you two did something other than have Willa Barton book club meetings?"

"Hell yeah." Brynn pointed to the shed. "That sucker is packed tight with fishing gear."

"Now that sounds more like the Dad and Brynn that I know..." Willa stopped herself when she realized that she no longer had her father in her life and she hardly knew anything about the person who Brynn was now.

Willa pulled herself forward on the bench and leaned as far up on her elbows as she could reach, hoping that she was far enough out of sight, so that Brynn wouldn't notice the glimmer of moisture forming at the corner of her eyes. She hoped that if she busied her mind by watching the ripples of water break along the surface of the sea, that she could control the forces of anger and sadness colliding inside of her. All she needed was a few moments to push her emotions back down where they could remain hidden.

The theory of her plan sounded perfect in her mind, but a hand rubbing her back in soothing circles, urging the sorrow to release, interrupted it. Willa turned on her seat as she swung one leg over so that she was straddling the bench. She took Brynn's hand from her back and cradled it into her hands where she could stare down at it, unable to look her in the face without breaking down completely.

"I don't deserve your sympathy," Willa choked out.

"Willa…"

"No, please let me explain why." Willa aimlessly tugged at Brynn's fingers while she formed the words that she needed to say. "While I appreciate more than you will ever understand, that you didn't treat me with the contempt that the rest of this town has shown me, you are the one person who I need the opposite from."

"I can't do that to you…"

The tears flowed freely from her eyes. "I'm begging you, please yell at me, blame me, hate me for what I've done to you."

Brynn pulled her hand away and Willa felt the

severed connection shatter her as sobs shook through her. It was temporary, though, as a finger lifted her chin and a thumb swiped away a river of tears down her cheek.

"Look at me." Brynn waited with a patient stillness until Willa's dark eyes blinked away enough of the hurt to lock onto her gaze. "It never once crossed my mind that you were to blame for this."

"But I pushed you."

"Because I kissed you." Brynn smiled and winked. "We can go back and forth like this all day."

Despite trying to hold onto the guilt that she was still overwhelmed with, Willa couldn't help but let a tiny bit of relief escape from her lips as they curved upward. She gripped onto the metal rim of the wheel between them and burrowed her face into Brynn's neck. She squeezed her eyes shut and took in the warmth that emanated from her skin. Brynn wrapped an arm around Willa's shoulders to pull her in closer and twisted her fingers into the long, thick strands of her curly hair. Together, they stayed in the tight embrace for many minutes. Willa's back was aching from being arched over, and the wheelchair tire was digging into her ribs, but she didn't dare move, not wanting to separate from what she had dreamed of doing for twenty years.

A soft voice broke the silence and whispered in Willa's ear. "Are you doing all right in there?"

Willa nodded into Brynn's neck with a little sigh and a frown. "I'm selfishly enjoying that you still smell like home."

"Home?"

"Mm-hmm," Willa's voice confirmed with a muffled sound that got lost in Brynn's neck. "You smell exactly like you always did, and I'm glad that it hasn't changed."

"There's still only one brand of bar of soap that you can buy at the Lighthouse General Store." Brynn nestled her nose into Willa's hair and inhaled. "You, on the other hand, smell very different than you used to."

Willa lifted her head and raised one of her eyebrows. "Do you not like it?"

"I didn't say that. It's just different." Brynn paused, the intensity of her thoughts showing through squinted eyes. "Fancy."

Willa giggled and pushed herself up off the wheel that was still lodged against her stomach. "So, when you attend those ridiculous Hollywood parties, they give you a gift bag filled with random cosmetics and perfumes. Recently, I got a bottle of shampoo which I fell in love with, so I ordered more of it, but when I got the bill, it was fifty dollars per bottle."

"Fifty bucks for a bottle of shampoo?"

"Yeah, I hope *fancy* is a good smell because I plan on using every single drop of that stuff until the bottle is dry."

Willa had always known Brynn to be so sure of herself in a confident way that she shared with her brother Griffin. They both had a sureness about them when it came to anything they said or did. Something changed now with Brynn, though, as she got quiet and she looked down in her lap. "Trust me, it's good, and worth every penny."

The heat rose in Willa's cheeks as she took in the view of the cove again, her fingers aimlessly flipping through the pages of the book that was in front of her on the table. A bookmark protruded from the top of it, about three quarters of the way to the end of the book. The thought swirled in her mind that her father would never get to know how the book ended, but she quickly pushed that idea out, knowing that she would encounter many more things that he would never get to do before her time of tying up loose ends for him was done. Instead, she held the book out to Brynn. "You should keep this, so that you can finish it."

"Thanks," Brynn said, placing it in the backpack along with the thermos and her empty mug. "I really should get back to the gym now."

"Of course." Willa stood and motioned to the entire clearing. "I appreciate you sharing this with me. It's a very special place that you two created here."

Brynn forced out a shaky smile and spun her wheelchair around to start up the wooden ramp. When Willa knew that Brynn couldn't see her, she exhaled deeply and covered her hand over her heart before following her up the hill.

The pure power in Brynn's arms showed as she pushed up the steady incline. Around corners, Willa could see as Brynn bit down on her lip and strained with each push on her wheels, before briskly reaching back to do it again, so as not to roll backwards. At times, Willa found herself reaching out, wanting to help Brynn with the strenuous process, but her wheelchair wasn't equipped with the handlebars on the back that Willa was used to seeing in hospitals. Hers was built to be as streamlined as possible, to be used for her vigorous athletic lifestyle. Willa knew that Brynn would never accept the help even if she needed it and so she held back and watched as Brynn wiped away the perspiration on her brow and pushed on to the top of the hill.

When they reached the parking lot again, Willa

placed a hand on Brynn's shoulder. "Do you have a minute to stop at my car? I have something that I want to give you."

Brynn tilted her head to the side and gave a lopsided grin. "Sure."

Willa reached into the passenger side seat of her car and pulled out a neatly folded shirt, which she handed to Brynn. Brynn held it up by the collar and let the shirt unravel open as she flipped it from front to back. "I'm surprised you were able to get the blood stains out of it."

Willa scrunched up her nose and bit anxiously at her fingertip. "I tried, but you're right, I couldn't get the stains out, no matter what I washed it with. I ended up ordering you a new one and had it express overnight delivered."

Brynn's eyes glimmered with a mischievous glare as she spun the shirt into a tight roll with a flick of her wrist, and flung one end of it like a whip towards Willa's hip. With a loud crack as it slapped against her thigh, a yelp from Willa, and the roaring laughter from Brynn, the empty parking lot exploded with sound.

"Ugh, I always hated it when you did that to me with beach towels." Willa playfully swatted her hand at Brynn, who batted it away with ease.

"Thanks for the shirt, but I really do have to go now."

Willa held out the lobster mug to Brynn. "Can you put this back in the locker for me? I'd like to do this again sometime before I leave Laurel Cove. If that's okay with you?"

"There's nothing I'd want more." Brynn waved her hand in the air as she sped off. "Until next time, Willa."

Chapter Twelve

Aunt Beth's SUV was parked in the driveway when Willa arrived back at her father's house. When she got out of the car, Beth waved from under the shade of an apple tree in the center of the front yard. Willa picked up a second folding chair from the front porch and joined her. "This is a surprise. I had no idea you were coming today."

"I received Henry's remains this afternoon, so I took a drive out to Laurel Cove to make arrangements at the chapel."

"Why didn't you call so that I could have been here when you arrived? I hope you weren't waiting long."

"No worries, dear. It's a beautiful day out and I had a good book to read." Beth patted the hard cover of a novel in her lap. "I'm ashamed to say that it's not one of yours, but the library had loaned your new one out before I got my hands on it."

"I'll mail you a copy so that you don't have to wait for it."

Beth reached out and tapped Willa's leg. "You'll do no such thing, my dear. Just between you and me, the librarian, Martin, and I have a little crush going on with each other. Bragging about my niece, the famous author, gives me something to talk about with him on our dinner dates."

"Ah, well, I wouldn't want to get in the way of

romance, now would I?" Willa winked playfully at her aunt. She leaned back in the chair and regarded the house for a moment. "You have a key to the house. You could have let yourself in, you know?"

"It didn't seem right to intrude. It's not my brother's home anymore. It belongs to you now."

Willa stared at the tiny house that she had dreamed of coming back to one day. For years, she had silently begged the universe to take back the events of the night that made her run from this place, so that she could return. Now that she was here, all that stood in front of her was an empty shell of a house filled with old material memories. "What kind of a home is it when the love is missing from it?"

Beth leaned over in her chair and gave Willa's wrist a squeeze. "Oh dear," she paused, "is there anyone in New York who you care for, someone special maybe?"

Willa shook her head. "Not really, no, there's no one," she said softly.

"There's definitely Barton blood running through those veins of yours. We all tend to be loners, but I've learned my lesson late in life, that love is better than loneliness. Know that I'm always here for you, but you need to create a family made up of people who aren't just blood. Build a family made up of friends, because those are the loved ones that you can truly count on when you need them the most."

"I'm trying, Aunt Beth. I think that for the first time I can actually say that I have a couple of friends now, so that's a start."

"Good for you. Will I get to meet them at the service tomorrow evening?"

"It's tomorrow?"

"Yes, there's no sense in dragging it out, as Henry

would say. I've followed through with everything on the list he left for me."

Beth pulled a folded piece of paper from under her book and handed it over to Willa. She opened it up and read:

Dear sis,

It seems a little strange, writing a letter for you to read after I've passed while I'm still alive and kicking, but my lawyer says it makes things easier for those I care about if I make it clear exactly what I want, so there's no guessing for you. All I ask is that you cremate me so that I don't have people gawking at my dead body, especially my girl. I'd hate to have her remember me like that. I never considered myself a man of God, but just in case, hold a little gathering at the chapel so that people can say their goodbyes. Watch over my Willa for me.

–Henry

Willa folded up the paper again and handed it back to Beth. She made a tight fist and held it up under her nose, pressing her knuckles against her lips. She bounced her long, slender leg up and down rapidly, not even noticing the pain from her stitches as the movement made them pull tight. The words written in his letter affected Willa in a way that she never imagined they would. She had set up the appointment for her father to make arrangements with a lawyer, many years ago out of a recommendation from her own advisor. He had agreed to it reluctantly, but never told her the details of what took place, just that it was all taken care of.

Willa never expected that he would have a handwritten letter for his family left behind. What bothered her the most was that she could almost hear his down east accent ringing out from the words on the page as she read it. The letter was short and to the point like his speech was when he was alive. He would spatter out little sentences filled with wisdom that was simple, but would come to Willa at times when she needed it the most. She could tell that the message in the letter held only the purpose to make sure that Beth did all the things that he thought his daughter shouldn't have to be burdened with. Even from the grave, he found a way to be a father to her.

Willa fidgeted uncomfortably in her seat, visibly fighting through the new series of emotions that the letter brought on. She was aware of Beth, silently waiting with patience as she worked through the sorrow. She wondered if it had been as painstakingly difficult for Beth the first time she read it too. Willa had become so accustomed to dealing with heartache on her own, though, that she turned away to conceal her pain.

"I wanted to wait and give you a little time to get reacquainted with things and people here in Laurel Cove again before giving you this, but I think it's best if you read the second half of Henry's request." Beth removed a second sheet of folded paper from the back of her book and slipped it onto Willa's lap.

The ink markings scrawled on the closed piece of paper spelled out her name. Willa recognized the handwriting from having seen it thousands of times throughout her life. Her father had marked just about everything that belonged to her with a piece of masking tape and a black pen with her name on it. It was the best way to ensure that she wouldn't accidentally grab the lunch bag in the refrigerator containing his liverwurst sandwich. Seeing it written on this piece of paper, though, had a sense of finality to it that disturbed her.

Willa looked to Beth with raised eyebrows and

Beth nodded her response, understanding that Willa needed a little privacy. She held out her hand for Beth to stay put, while she stood and leaned her body against the trunk of the apple tree, faced in the opposite direction to offer herself some space.

Willa unfolded the paper and her eyes were already glazed over with tears before she began to read:

My dearest Willa,

I don't want to be stuck in a box in the ground, so I'd like to be spread at sea where I belong with the fish. If I can't catch 'em, I may as well feed 'em. Now, I know you might not like this next request, but I'd hope you'd do your best to make it happen for me. I want you, Brynn, and Griffin to take my ashes out on the boat for one last ride to the open ocean and let me go there. This will be difficult for you, to say the least, I know, but set me up on the mantle and bring me out to sea in your own good time when the three of you can set aside your differences long enough to make this old man proud of his favorite people. You have always been the beacon to my lighthouse.

–Dad

Willa swiped away the loose tears running down her face with the back of her wrist. "Did you read this?" she asked, holding up the letter, but not wanting to turn and face her aunt quite yet.

"No, it had your name on it, not mine. It was meant only for you and I kept it that way. I did, however, talk to Henry about it soon after he wrote it. He wanted me to be aware of the decisions he made so that I could help you through the process. So yes, I know exactly what he's asking of you."

Willa pushed around the mulch at the base of the tree with the tip of her sneaker. The overgrown grass required mowing soon and her father had always taken great pride in keeping his yard looking presentable. She had never actually used a lawnmower before because her father had always taken care of it here, and her New York condominium didn't have grass, similar to most of the high-rise buildings in the city. She wondered if she could figure out how to get the mower in the shed started, or if she should hire someone to do it for her.

The creaking of the lawn chair behind her brought Willa out of her wandering thoughts. She knew that she was mentally procrastinating against what she would have to do to carry out her father's last wish. The only other person alive in the world who knew what she needed to do, besides the lawyer, was sitting a few feet away from her and she felt somehow obligated to defend herself against her own apprehension. "Regardless of how I feel about doing this, Dad had no idea how much anger Griffin has towards me. If this is the only way he wants it done, he will never be laid to rest."

"From the stories that Henry used to tell me, he spent a lot of his time with both of those people in your absence. I find it difficult to believe that they wouldn't be willing to fulfill a simple request out of a respect for the man you all cared for."

Willa returned to the chair, but instead of sitting, she rested her hands on the back of it, hung her head down between her arms, and blew out an exasperated breath. "It won't be a simple task to convince Griffin that this is for my dad and not for me."

Beth pinched Willa's cheek on the way past her, just as she did when she was a child. "I'm sure you'll find a way through to him. A man never truly loses the affections he had once, for his first love as a boy."

She made her way over to her car but before closing her door she added, "A good place to start would be to invite him to the service tomorrow."

She waved goodbye to her aunt, grateful that her father had entrusted someone to help her with all the arrangements that came with planning a funeral.

Chapter Thirteen

*B*ent over the lawnmower and peering inquisitively into the open gas tank, Willa didn't hear as Megan stepped into the opening of the shed door.

"Did you drop something down there?"

Willa stood up at the sound of Megan's voice. She had a pair of carpenter's kneepads on both of her legs and bright yellow rubber gloves, meant for washing dishes, were pulled up past her elbows. "I can't seem to find an indicator that shows how much gasoline is in the tank."

"There isn't usually a gauge for that on small mowers, only the riding ones. You sort of eyeball it when it gets close to the surface." Megan picked up the red metal gas can and started to pour it. "See how you can tell that it's almost full, because it's starting to come up into the neck of the tank." Willa watched the process closely, scrunching up her nose when the fumes escaped into the air. Megan set the gas can aside and Willa screwed the cap back on until it clicked into place.

"Like a car, these things need oil changes every once in a while, but if your father kept his tools in as good a condition as he did his boat, you should be all set."

"I tried to find a video on the internet on how to start this thing up, but it's an older model, and there wasn't any information on it out there, not even an owner's manual." Willa shook her head and stuck out her bottom lip.

"My landscaper for The Anchor is really good. I can give you his number."

"I thought about going that route, but my dad took a lot of pride in maintaining his yard. I think he'd be disappointed in me trusting a stranger to take care of it. I'd like to at least attempt to keep it up myself while I'm here."

"Okay, well, let's roll it out to the lawn, before I teach you how to start it."

At the edge of the driveway, where the black tar met the blades of grass, Willa rubbed her rubber glove clad hands together in anticipation on learning something new.

Megan rolled her eyes at Willa's choice of accessories. "You do know that everyone who lives on the Cove has to drive by here to get to just about anywhere else?"

She leaned over and knocked on one of the kneepads with her knuckles. "Something has to protect my stitches while I do yard work." She raised her hands in the air and wiggled her fingers in the in gloves, "and I doubt there's a respectable manicurist anywhere on this island."

"You've got a point there. Just let me be the one to get a photograph of you to sell to the tabloid magazines. If anyone's going to make a buck off your embarrassing outfit, it better be me."

Willa stuck her tongue out and poked Megan's arm in jest. "Come on, show me how to run this thing before someone really does see me out here dressed like a lunatic."

"All right, the first step is to press this button." Megan placed her finger on an unmarked red button on the side of the lawnmower, pushed it in, and released it a few times.

"Nothing happened. Do you think it's broken?"

Megan laughed. "That doesn't turn it on. It primes the engine before you start it."

Willa's forehead crinkled up and she shifted from leg to leg while examining what the button might possibly be attached to behind it. "You pressed it more than once. Exactly how many times should I press it? What happens if I press it too many times?"

"Whoa, relax, there isn't a test at the end of this lesson, Ms. Valedictorian." Megan flashed her a reassuring grin and Willa took the comment as the joke it was meant to be.

"Ha." Willa let out a timid snicker. "Everyday life experiences become lessons for writers. I'm constantly being tested by my readers and they have no problem letting me know when I haven't accurately described the slightest of details in a story."

"In that case, I better get this right for the next time you write that great American novel about mowing a lawn. Three pushes on the primer when you haven't used it in a while and more if it's colder outside."

Megan drew back on a metal bar and held it against the handle of the lawnmower, then she stepped aside so that Willa could take her place.

"What happens if I let go of the bar?"

"It stops the motor, so release it when you're done. To start it, keep the bar in place with one hand and use the other one to pull on this cord." Megan pointed to a handle on the base of the mower.

She looked down at where the handle was located

and it seemed like an awkward position to hold onto something up high, while simultaneously pulling on another thing down below. She readjusted her body so that she could reach both a little more easily, and then she tugged on the cord. It made a whirring noise, but immediately came to a silent halt when the cord settled back into place.

"It might take a couple of tries," Megan mentioned after seeing the confused look on her face. "Put a little more power into it this time."

After a few more attempts and a short break in between to tie her hair back from her face, the engine finally roared to life. Her eyes widened when she felt the power of the machine vibrating in her hands.

Megan waved her arms in the air, but Willa was unable to hear her over the spinning of the blades, so Megan pointed to the expanse of the lawn. Willa followed her cue to start moving and made a straight line along the edge of the driveway with the mower. She stopped when she reached the wooden fence at the end and let go of the lever to shut it down. When she glanced back at the neatly trimmed path that she had created, Willa raised her arms up in triumph and rushed over to embrace Megan and let out an excited squeal. "It works!" She shook Megan's shoulders and a delighted grin spread across her face. "I couldn't have done it without you."

"Well, I'm glad that I could help you out with your little predicament, but now how about you tell me the real reason why you called me over?"

Willa bowed her head down and slowly removed the gloves from her hands. She sucked the corner of her bottom lip into her mouth and let it fall back out. "The grass was getting out of control..." Willa looked down at it as if it were a major problem.

"Oh please, every man, woman, and child on this island could have helped show you how to run a damn lawnmower. I can tell that hidden under this homemaker outfit, you are secretly freaking out about something, which is why you contacted me. It's my duty as your friend to know when you need to talk."

Willa withered to the ground like a deflated balloon and sat with her legs outstretched along the strip of freshly cut grass. "Ugh, you're right, everything's a mess."

Megan dropped down across from Willa and flashed her a sympathetic look. "*Everything* sounds like a bit of an exaggeration. Let's start with the biggest issue you have and see if I can help you work through that one first."

"My deceased father expects me to spread his ashes in the middle of the ocean, but only when I am prepared to do it in the company of both Brynn and Griffin."

Megan stared back at her with raised eyebrows, wide eyes, and mouth dropped down open so far that her jaw looked like it was detached.

"That was exactly my reaction," Willa said after a lack of a verbal response from Megan, "but maybe with a little more anger and sadness thrown in."

"Sorry, I just wasn't expecting that at all."

"Neither was I. It was sort of sprung on me right before I called you. Everything I had planned on accomplishing during my time here will have to be put on hold until I can figure this out."

"Are you going to try to do something about this before you leave Laurel Cove?"

"I have to. The only way that the three of us will

be able to do this together is if I can somehow get Griff to communicate with me, and I can't get through to him over the phone with two other states between us, when it's already intimidating to get him to speak to me in person."

Megan placed her hand up in midair. "Back up a second. You only mentioned Griffin. Does that mean things went well with Brynn today?"

Willa tried her best to conceal the whimsical grin that turned up at the corners of her lips, along with the pink coloring that was rising up in her cheeks. "Talking to Brynn again is like being back in my old house; it's comforting and scary all at the same time."

"Why scary?"

She ran her fingers across the top of a patch of uncut grass and plucked a blade from it. "I can't help but wonder if she's only being civil to me because she knows how badly I'm hurting right now."

"Don't allow yourself to think that way. If she still held a grudge against you, she wouldn't be able to fake it no matter what the circumstance."

"I hope you're right; she holds as many memories of my father as I do, if not more. If I lost her, it would be like losing the last piece of him that I have left."

"It seems like Griffin might also share some of that history."

Willa scrunched up her nose and rubbed at her forehead as if it was physically painful to accept the truth that Megan was facing her with. "He does."

"Regardless of what your father is requesting to be done, don't you want to fix things between you and Griffin?"

"Other than Brynn, he was the very best friend that I've ever had. If there is any possibility of us reconciling our differences at all, I'll do what I must, because I miss him dearly."

"Then you need to try, not just for your father's sake, but for your own."

"Any suggestions on how I can get him to stop being so angry at me for a few minutes so that I can talk to him?"

"In a case like that, let him be angry because it's probably the only way he knows how to show that he's hurt. If he sees that you aren't willing to give up on him, then eventually, he might back down and listen."

Willa rose up slowly, favoring the tenderness of her injured leg, and held out a hand to help Megan to her feet. Before she could step away, Willa pulled her into an embrace. "Thank you for coming to my rescue today, for both the mower and the advice."

Megan gave her a tight squeeze and then held her at arm's length so that she could look her in the eyes. "Promise me that you'll back off if Griffin's anger becomes a danger to you, okay?"

"I promise."

Chapter Fourteen

By the time Willa had completed the yard work that she started and cleaned up the copious amounts of grass clippings and dirt that had found a place to stick to her body, the sun had already set. She made a few phone calls to distant acquaintances whom Willa knew would want to attend the funeral service. As far as the rest of the tiny island, the news would spread like rapid fire from person to person until everyone was aware of the ceremony tomorrow.

Willa paced the length of the living room while contemplating what to do about getting the message out to Brynn and Griffin. She was more than certain that they would know by now, especially with patrons of their gym passing through, but she felt as though they were both owed the decency of being told in person. Her aunt had paid her the respect enough to tell her face to face and she intended to do the same for them, once she worked up the nerve enough to do it. The pacing continued while she ran scenarios of what might be said repeatedly in her head as if she were writing out the dialog of conversations in one of her stories. The problem was that, unlike the fiction she wrote, she could control what she said, but not what Griffin would.

The ride to the gym took less time than she had hoped for, even going way under the speed limit that was already low due to the narrow, winding roads.

This was one of those times when she wouldn't have minded one of the hectic city traffic jams that she usually cursed at on her daily commute.

Even after all of the mental preparations she had set herself up with, she silently hoped that Brynn would still be alone at the gym and that she could pass the information on to Griffin without having to talk to him. Willa tugged at the metal handle of the gym's door a couple of times and it still didn't budge. Confused, she went to the closest window where she could see that the lights were all on and a few people were scattered about, using various exercise equipment throughout the spacious room. She returned to the door and tried once again, but it still wouldn't open. When she raised her fist up to knock on it, in hopes of possibly getting the attention of someone without earphones in, she noticed the engraved sign above the handle that read: *after hours use the keypad for entry.*

"Ugh," Willa grunted in frustration as she made her way back to the car in the parking lot. There was only one place where she could find both of the twins, but going to their house without an invitation from Griffin was like begging for a nasty confrontation.

The Reed's house was hardly a few seconds drive down the road from the gym and that was if Willa coasted without accelerating. Before she knew it, she was turning into their driveway without having really given herself enough time to decide if that was what she actually wanted to do. Once the car was in park, she figured that she was fully committed to executing this visit, so she glanced in the rearview mirror out of habit, to check her makeup. There wouldn't be any unexpected camera flashes as she exited her vehicle, but it would always be ingrained in her to maintain a certain image status for the occasions when it did matter.

The last time that Willa had been at this house, there was a line of flat stones that created a quaint path surrounded by flowers, which led up to the porch. All of that had been removed to make room for the ramp that now consumed most of that space. She slowly made her way towards the front of the house, but the second that her foot touched the ramp, a motion detector triggered a light system, illuminating the entire front yard in a bright hue. Willa let out an annoyed moan at the thought that her arrival would not go unnoticed at this point, and she wouldn't have a few precious moments to collect her thoughts before ringing the bell. In fact, her hand didn't even have time to reach out for the button, when the door opened.

To Willa's relief, it was Brynn at the door, and she couldn't help but feel breathless when a giant smile spread across Brynn's face. When she saw what was laying across her lap, Willa's eyes widened and she retreated a couple of steps.

"Oh, geez." Brynn gasped when she noticed what Willa was so scared of. She lifted the gun off her legs and made a show of setting it carefully down on a side table before she rolled out onto the porch and silently shut the door behind her. "It's just a pellet gun that shoots off rubber ammo. The groundhogs have been relentlessly eating everything in the vegetable garden this summer and I thought it was one of them that set off the lights out here."

"I shouldn't have come over unannounced." Willa twisted her set of car keys up in a ball along with the key chain, intertwining them with her fingers. She unconsciously began backing up further as if she were going to leave.

Brynn eyed Willa's reservations, quickly pulled a plastic chair away from a patio table, and patted the seat on it. "Sit with me for a while and tell me why you stopped by."

Willa reluctantly hovered over the chair for a few seconds and surveyed the view of the interior of the house from the window. The lights were on, but there was no sign of Griffin moving around inside. "I came by to tell you about the funeral," she said while easing herself down uncomfortably on the edge of the seat, prepared to get up when needed, at a moment's notice.

"Griff has no idea that you're here. He's down in the basement lifting weights," Brynn said with a reassuring smile.

"Some things never change, huh?" Willa settled further back into the chair, but left her leg firmly in place where it was slightly brushing up against Brynn's leg. Willa understood that Brynn wouldn't feel the protection that she did in their connection, unless she visibly caught a glimpse of their touch. "It's uh, it's tomorrow evening at the chapel."

"We know already. Griff heard about it when he closed up Mussels for the night, from someone that had been down at the docks earlier today."

"Good, good, I wanted you both to know because he would want you there." The words came out of her mouth, but her gaze was lost up towards the night sky, along with her thoughts.

Brynn took a hold of Willa's hand, pulling her back to their conversation. "How are you holding up through all of this?"

Willa exhaled slowly, letting her cheeks puff out in the process. "It's like everything is moving so fast around me. Mostly, I'm scared that I'm not prepared to say goodbye so soon, but I can't anyway because he's already gone."

Brynn leaned in closer and took Willa's hand into her own lap, then began gently rubbing the top of it with her thumb. "If there's anything I can do to help ease your pain, know that I'm here for you." The offer that Brynn made caused Willa's heart to swell with empathy for Brynn, whom she knew was grieving as much as she was. With a lack of words between them, they found contentment in the stillness of the night and solace in the contact of each other's hands.

Their tranquil connection was severed hastily, though, when the front door flung open and Griffin stepped out into their quiet sanctuary. They silently watched as he scanned the front yard with difficulty as his eyes adjusted to the dimly lit porch.

"Hey, sis, are you out here?" he called out, but his own question was answered when he peered away from the lawn and back to the porch.

Willa stood, the force knocking the flimsy plastic chair over on its back. She hadn't meant to pull herself away from Brynn's grasp so harshly, but the hulking figure of Griffin taking up more space than the frame of the doorway provided caused her to back away more abruptly than she intended.

"What are you doing at my house?" His chest protruded out and his shoulders raised up above his neckline.

"It's *our* house and she's my guest." Brynn rolled up in the narrow space that the porch provided, putting herself between Griffin and Willa.

Willa averted her eyes to the ground and held her hand out in front of her, not wanting to cause a conflict between the siblings. "I only came to make sure that you were aware of the service tomorrow."

Griffin tilted his head down at an angle faced away from them and ever so minutely softened the tone of his voice. "We already know."

Willa reached out past Brynn and let her fingertips lightly brush against his shirt. "Griff…" The words she wanted to say got stuck somewhere in her throat.

He swatted her hand away. "You're not welcome here."

"Don't be an ass," Brynn snapped at him.

Willa stopped Brynn by placing the palm of her hand against her chest. "It's okay, he's right, I shouldn't have come here."

Willa heard Brynn call out her name, but she had already reached her car door and slammed it shut before Brynn and Griffin had a chance to argue over whether she should stay or go. She knew them well enough to know that when they disagreed on something, it was best to leave them alone to work out their problem, which in this case was her. She hoped that by removing herself from the equation that things would settle down between them. She was in such a hurry to escape from the crossfires of the twins, though, that she took the wrong turn out at the end of their driveway and ended up continuing until she reached the end of the cove.

A small dirt lot that served as a parking area was the last stop before the road ended and the sea began. Willa planned on turning around here instead of in someone's yard, but when she found that it was empty, she parked her car. The only people who ever used this space were tourists and teenagers from the surrounding mainland towns looking for a romantic location to bring a date. The locals all had their own private spots and they tended to stay away from this beach, which was why Willa decided that tonight, this was exactly where she belonged. Her out of state license plate, and car that cost more than most homes on this island, fit in perfectly in the lot meant for tourists, but mostly her heart felt out of place.

A steep, narrow path wound down to the sandy beach below. The tide was full, which left very little space between the water and the rocky cliff surrounding the beach. Willa swept a clump of dried seaweed off a driftwood log and settled down on it. Even in the darkness of the night, the moon and stars reflected off the ocean and everything seemed to sparkle with light. Willa convinced herself that the only dark place in the world that night was deep within her own heart.

Chapter Fifteen

The little chapel was packed full to capacity with people, well before the service was due to begin. With the exception of a few elderly parishioners who attended the church regularly, no one was quite sure what religion was practiced within the holy walls of the building. It was just a fact that every wedding and funeral on Laurel Cove took place there no matter what their religious beliefs were.

Willa sat on a wooden bench behind a curtain, in a small room specifically reserved as a place for direct family members to have private time alone when they needed it. She couldn't help but think about how brides also used this space, where they waited with their father until it was time to walk down the aisle. She added that event to the list of things she would never share with her own father. People's most joyful and sorrowful moments mixed with the energy of the room. Just the thought of that made Willa dizzy.

She wondered if her dad had held her in his arms when she was a toddler, in this very room, as her mother's funeral was taking place. She had a few select memories of her mother, but being in the chapel for her service was not one of them. It was most likely the beginning of one of the many times in her life when her father had shielded her from the sadness of the day by covering it up with his infectious smiles and love.

She peeled aside a portion of the red velvet curtain

to peer across the hall where people were filing in the rows of pews. A constant murmur vibrated amongst the crowd. Conversations were spoken in whispers too low for her to pick up on what was being said, but by the solemn expressions on their faces, they genuinely seemed to be as upset about her father being gone as she was. Until seeing for herself how many lives he had interwoven his own with in their tiny community, she had never given much thought as to how missed he would be.

When a silence fell throughout the building, the minister, who to Willa seemed to be as old as time itself, came to get her. He held a frail hand out to help her from the bench. When she took it, his skin looked so white and thin that it almost appeared to be translucent. He led her past the curtain to a small group of people, all of which were dressed in robes and carried religious objects to be part of the ceremony. A silver urn was placed in Willa's hands and for the first time, she realized that she was expected to carry her father's remains down to the front of the church. She shook her head to deny the responsibility, and held the urn out for someone else to take it, but it was too late; the line had already begun its procession towards the altar.

Organ music echoed throughout the chapel, masking the pounding in her chest, which Willa was so convinced that everyone would be able to hear otherwise. An altar boy signaled that it was her turn to follow behind him, when she obviously left too large of a gap after he had gone, and so she took her first few steps down the aisle. To Willa's horror, everyone stood and turned in her direction to face her. She vowed that after this experience ended, she would never scoff at having to walk down a red-carpet event ever again.

The first pew that she went by, located in the very back, had Brynn positioned on the end closest to the aisle, because it was the only wheelchair accessible spot in the church. Willa glanced down at her briefly as she passed, but the bright blue of her eyes were clouded with darkness and filled with sorrow. It was too much for her to bear, so Willa forced herself to look away. If she hoped to make it to the altar without withering into a hysterical mess, she had to focus on the intricate designs of the urn in her hands instead of the people surrounding her.

Placing the urn on a pedestal was as nerve wracking as picking up a newborn baby for the first time, and the audience behind her made it even more terrifying. Through sweating palms, trembling fingers, and a dizzy mind, she somehow managed to steady the urn onto the tiny square platform. In a haze of confusion, she searched for guidance on what her next move should be. The lector motioned for her to take a seat in the first pew, which, to her surprise, was completely empty. There wasn't an available space in the entire church, and yet she was secluded from everyone.

The only person with a blood relation to her was her aunt, and Beth sat behind Willa, holding the hand of a man that she assumed was the librarian that she had spoken of the day before. The seat was hard and cold and Willa didn't think that she could handle the idea of everyone's eyes on the back of her head during the most miserable hour of her life. She turned and searched the crowd until the first familiar face she noticed came into her line of vision.

Shannon flashed her a supportive, yet serious

smile. Willa shook her head slightly, to show that she needed more than just that from her. She leaned over the back of the pew and held her hand out, palm up, to invite her over to sit with her. Shannon nodded and excused herself as she slipped past a row of people that had to push their knees aside for her to pass, and continued on to take a seat next to Willa. She leaned her head in close to Shannon's ear. "Thank you," she said as she let her face rest on Shannon's shoulder.

The organ music suddenly came to a dramatic end and the rustling of the crowd settled to an eerie silence. The minister raised his hands up and closed his eyes in preparation. A clicking sound of heels on the wooden floor approaching them caused Willa to lift her head up. Megan was hunched over, attempting to be as inconspicuous as possible, but failing, as she was the only one moving around in the completely silent church. The minister glared at her as he held off on beginning the ceremony until she was seated. Megan had a hold of her daughter Ava's hand, and nudged Willa to slide over to make room for them on the pew.

The minister pushed his glasses up on the bridge of his nose and raised his eyebrows at Willa, as if he were asking her to cease with the distractions. She glanced to her newly created support system of friends by her side and bowed her head for him to begin. The minister's voice was anything but frail as it boomed so loudly that it could be felt deep inside those within the chapel's walls. "We have gathered here today in remembrance of our dear friend and family member, Henry Barton." Those were the only words that Willa paid attention to throughout the entire service. There were times when she followed the motions of others around her, such as when to kneel on the narrow wooden board at her feet, which Shannon was sure to pad down with her sweater, under the knee with the stitches on it. There was also a time when they stood in line to eat the wafer that tasted to her like a stale piece of cardboard. For the rest of the time, she focused on the silky fabric of her designer pants suit, one that her father had commented on liking when he saw it in a photograph that a fan took at a book signing.

Time flew by so swiftly that Willa wasn't even sure what was happening when Megan prodded her side to stand up again. She promptly figured out that it was time for her to carry the urn back out again. The words spoken during the ceremony, although lost upon Willa's ears, had clearly affected the rest of the crowd, because there were many tear streaked faces amongst them. The sight of their pain, mixed with the background music from the organ and the hauntingly sad voices of the choir singers, brought on the tears that she had worked so diligently at holding back. She didn't dare move one of her trembling hands from either side of the urn to swipe the tears away, so she lowered her head and rushed down the aisle, practically pushing her way around the procession line in front of her. When she believed that there was no possible way to escape the scrutiny of everyone's stares, a pair of hands reached up and took the burden of the urn from her.

Traditionally, Willa was supposed to wait at the rear of the chapel as people walked by and offered their condolences, but she had no desire to torture herself further with this parade of pain she felt like she was taking part in. Instead, she went straight for the exit and rushed out to her car. Willa's fingers fumbled in her pockets for her keys, but during the process of trying to unlock it, she accidentally hit the alarm button. Between water filled eyelids and fingers that shook uncontrollably, she couldn't find the right button to stop the shrieking horn honking and flashing headlights, both of which were drawing all the attention she was attempting to avoid in her direction.

An arm wrapped around Willa's waist and helped ground her so that the feeling of helplessness subsided from her body. The keys, held so tight in her fist that they would leave imprints a long time afterwards, were removed from her hand and the alarm stopped. A tiny click sound released the locks on the car doors, and the arm around her waist gently guided her down into the driver's seat. With her feet dangling out of her open car door and mascara running down her face, Willa stuck out her lower lip and sniffled. "I made a total fool of myself in there, didn't I?"

Brynn swiped away the dark lines streaming down Willa's cheeks with her thumb. "Nah, you just look like a daughter mourning the loss of her dad."

"Oh no, what if someone took a photo of me? I look horrible. The media could attach any kind of story they wanted to a picture like that."

"You don't have to worry about that here. The island is like a big family, a highly dysfunctional one, but a family nonetheless. Besides, even at your very worst, you're still gorgeous."

A blush swept over Willa's face and to take the attention away from it, she gave Brynn's shin a playful tap with the tip of her high-heeled shoe. She didn't even have time to pull her foot back, when she realized what she had done. Her teeth bit down and a hiss came out as she grimaced.

Upon seeing Willa's reaction, Brynn covered the

spot where Willa had kicked with her hand. "Ow," she said rubbing the spot.

Willa's eyes widened and she reached down to cover the injured location with her palm. "I'm so sorry," she said with a frown.

Brynn's chuckling stopped Willa's apology from going on any longer. "I couldn't help myself." She knocked her knuckles lightly on her leg a few times with her fist. "Can't feel a thing down there, remember?"

Willa narrowed her eyes. "That is so not funny," she said, dragging each syllable out to make her point clear.

"It's a joke in bad taste, I know, but it did get you to forget how sad you were a minute ago, didn't it?"

Willa couldn't resist the bright blue eyes practically begging for forgiveness. She had almost forgotten over the years of just how much of a prankster her best friend had always been. "You *always* cheer me up, Brynn. Thank you for that, and for coming to my rescue, yet again."

Brynn's face lit up, and Willa was glad that they could both be alleviated from some of the pain that the loss of a loved one brings, but a sinking feeling swept over her once more as a shadow loomed above them.

"It's time to go, Brynn," Griffin announced as he leaned in over the open door.

Willa pulled her legs into the car as she retreated away from the secluded little space that she had made with Brynn.

"Back off," Brynn said sternly, not even bothering to turn her attention to him.

Griffin made a show of putting his hands in the air as he let go of the door and slowly walked away. "I'm heading out now and there's no way your chair will fit in the back of that tiny chunk of metal that she flaunts around in."

Brynn shook her head at his comment. "Ignore him; he's having a difficult day too, even though he'll never admit it."

Someone else approached them, but this time, to Willa's relief, it was Shannon.

"Because there's no burial, everyone's looking for a place to gather to offer up their condolences. I figured you didn't have anything planned, so I spread the word that they could meet at my house, if that's okay with you?"

"That's very kind of you." Willa reached out and squeezed her wrist. "I appreciate your help."

"Of course. I need to get home, because people are sure to be showing up soon. Come by when you're ready." Shannon rushed off into the crowd of people in the parking lot. Willa nodded and wondered if she would ever really be ready to attend a social event with a group of people who were hardly even considered acquaintances, and discuss how much they missed her father.

"Are you going to be there?"

Brynn looked down at the urn still in her lap and frowned. "I don't think it would be a good idea to bring Griff there and I don't want to leave him today. It's like we lost another father all over again."

"I understand."

Brynn placed her hand on the top of the urn and closed her eyes for a second. Willa watched as Brynn said her silent goodbye to Henry, then she carefully handed it over to Willa. "Take Dad home and then get to Shannon's so that you won't be alone tonight."

"I will." Willa lingered for a moment, not wanting

to leave just yet. "It was nice seeing you again, even if it was in the worst of circumstances."

"You too." Brynn paused and then a huge grin swept over her face. "Hey, Griff is leaving to visit Mom in Florida tomorrow afternoon. There's a weightlifting competition down south, so he'll be gone for most of the week. Would you want to spend some time together?"

"More than anything."

Chapter Sixteen

Willa drove back to the house slowly and cautiously, treating her father's remains as precious as a newborn infant's first ride. She had strapped the silver urn in the passenger seat with the safety belt in fear that it might slide off the seat if she had to come to a sudden stop. It wasn't until she had him settled upon the mantle in the living room, as he had requested, that she was able to be at ease.

With a vague anticipation of the events that might occur at Shannon's house later, Willa removed her contacts, wiped away any trace of what remained of her severely smudged mascara, and put on her glasses. If she were to shed any more tears, she wanted to do it with slightly more dignity than before. The glasses, even though they provided nothing more than a false sense of security, still felt like a shield to her.

Rows of vehicles lined the edges of both sides of the road leading up to Shannon's house. Judging by the sheer number of them, it seemed as though just about everyone that had attended the service had chosen to gather here. Willa was thankful for the compact size of her car now, because there was a space large enough for her to park at the end of the driveway. She shuddered when she pictured herself having to walk all that way on the side of the road in high heels.

Inside the house, Willa noticed Shannon was standing in front of an oil painting displayed on her living room wall. A group of people were surrounding her and admiring the artwork as she described the particular brush strokes the artist used to create it. When she caught sight of Willa, she excused herself from the others and came over to greet her. "How are you holding up?"

Willa held out her hand and waved it diagonally a few times. "It would have been a lot worse if I had to host something like this at the last minute back at the house. I wouldn't have been prepared at all."

"I don't think it occurred to your Aunt Beth either, until she saw the turnout at the chapel. Her house is too far away on the mainland, and tiny from the description she gave me. Besides, I literally know every person here," Shannon motioned to two elderly women as they reminisced over a photograph of three generations of doctors in the Martin family, "and I think they're starting to see me as a person instead of just a healthcare provider."

Willa smiled warmly. "I'm glad that something positive is coming from this."

"If you need some time to yourself at all, go to the second room on the left down the hall. It's a spare bedroom with its own bathroom so you can step away from the chaos momentarily."

"Thank you. Is there anything I can help you with?"

"No, I'm going to fill some pitchers with ice water. You should mingle with the guests, though; you'd be surprised at how many stories of your father they have. He was a beloved man in the community."

Willa nodded and crossed her arms in front of herself, pretending to rub at the cold on her skin even though it was quite warm inside, especially with the large number of people gathered there. Social events for Willa consisted of book signings, movie premieres, and awards ceremonies. People attending them were either fellow colleagues in the industry or fans of her work. It was all too easy, and often times annoying, to start up a conversation with just about anyone who surrounded her. Complete strangers seemed to know details about her life and used that information to converse as if they had known each other for years. She dodged those sorts of people at events, and yet at this particular moment, she would have appreciated the attention that they showered her with. Old feelings resurfaced as if she were once again the socially awkward bookworm that she had been back in high school.

She decided, after scanning the room, that she would embrace the one thing she knew the most about and check out the bookshelves that lined one wall of the living room. An elderly woman with her head tilted to one side was reading the spines of a row of books, so Willa took a spot near her to start looking. It became evident after examining more than one shelf that every book had something to do with the human body. There were countless books on anatomy, the skeletal system, the circulatory system, blood, and many other detailed medical textbooks on subjects of the body that she had never even heard of before. The closest thing that she could find that even resembled a story was a book of personal accounts of doctors in emergency room situations. Willa pulled it down from the shelf and flipped through the pages. She skimmed a few of the stories, but they were quite gruesome in the details and they made her cringe. "Gross," she said, scrunching up her nose and placing the book back on the shelf.

"Oh my, the subject matter of these books is less than desirable, unless you're a doctor, of course," the elderly woman said, taking a step closer to Willa.

Willa looked up from the book about the human brain that she was currently browsing through. "I couldn't imagine having to memorize all of this information for college either. No wonder so few students make it through medical school."

"We are quite fortunate that Dr. Martin followed in her father's footsteps and took over his practice. Without her, we would have to travel to the mainland for every injury and sickness we had."

"I never thought about that. Wouldn't another doctor have purchased the clinic if she hadn't wanted to?"

"And have to put up with life out here, and people like us? No, you have to be from here to want to stay. Half of the people who own the summer homes on the Cove are doctors from out of state, but they know well enough to be gone by snowfall so that they don't have to endure our harsh winters."

Willa bit at her lip and hugged the hardbound book to her chest. "I learned the difficult way that when you do leave, you realize that there is no other place that compares to this," she said softly.

"That's because you're one of us, dear, and you always will be, just like your father."

"May I ask how you knew him?"

"We only spoke a time or two, but if it wasn't for both him and Dr. Martin, my grandson wouldn't be alive today."

Willa looked at the woman with narrowed eyes. She most certainly had never heard any stories of her father and Shannon doing anything together, much less saving a life. "Are you sure it was Henry Barton that saved your grandson?"

"Oh yes, it was him, for certain." She pushed her bifocal glasses that had been seated at the tip of her nose up, and blinked her wrinkle-encircled eyes into focus before starting the story. "Last summer, a storm had come in faster than expected and my daughter called to tell me that Ethan was still out fishing in his kayak. I live close to the docks so I rushed over, but all of lobster boats had gotten in early to avoid the storm. The only man left down there was Henry. He went right back out and found Ethan overturned and hanging on for dear life to his kayak. He had taken in some water in his lungs and had a touch of hypothermia, but your father got him over to Dr. Martin in time to help him until the ambulance came in from the mainland."

Willa's thoughts drifted as she envisioned the events of that day, and how brave her dad had been to go back out into a storm alone. "He never told me that story."

"That's because he's a humble man disguised in a hero's body."

Willa smiled. She had always thought that about him, but she assumed that every little girl felt that way about her father. It was something altogether different to hear it come from a stranger, though. "Thank you for sharing the story with me and I'm glad your grandson is okay."

The woman didn't appear to be paying attention to her as she eyed the activity near the front door. "The hors d'oeuvres have arrived. I do hope there's something sweet in there." She took off fast despite her feeble legs, which looked barely strong enough to hold her up, in the direction of someone carrying a stack of trays.

A few locks of red hair bounced out from behind the containers and Willa rushed over to help take a couple of layers off the pile in Megan's arms. She tried her best to ignore the fact that the old woman was lifting the corner up on one of the trays to sneak a cookie out from under it, before she could find a place to set them down. Megan motioned towards the dining room with her nose and Willa hurried to the table when she noticed that people from all over were now flocking towards them to help themselves to a snack.

"Where did you get all of this?" Willa asked as she removed the covers off trays filled with deli meats, slices of cheese, vegetable assortments, and tiny desserts.

"I had them made up at The Anchor when Shannon mentioned that she was having a gathering at her house. People expect snacks at these things."

"There is *so* much food here. Make sure that you put the cost of these on my tab at the restaurant."

Megan waved off Willa's request as if it were not important. "Don't be silly."

Willa furrowed her brow and spoke in a stern voice, "I'm not kidding, Meg; I'd better see the full amount on my bill."

"I promise," she said with a defiant glare.

"Something tells me you're just trying to appease me, but either way, I'm reimbursing you for all of this." Willa reached for a brownie, but before she could pick it up, Megan slapped her hand away. Willa looked at her with wide eyes and an open mouth.

Megan pulled out a square package, neatly wrapped in brown paper and secured with a piece of twine wound around it, and handed it to Willa. "I made you a sandwich because I figured that you probably haven't eaten anything all day."

"How do you seem to know me so well?"

"Oh hon, this would be a difficult day for anyone in your situation."

"That's true, but your friendship has been a blessing throughout all of this."

Chapter Seventeen

Ith all of the people still lingering at Shannon's house, Willa found that she was spending most of her time in the presence of Megan, which was not part of her plan to get to know people who her father associated with. When she noticed a man around her father's age sitting alone at the patio table, she brought out a couple of glasses of ice water and joined him. The man tipped the rim of his ball cap in thanks and pushed a plate of cookies in her direction.

"I think I have room for one more of these before I burst," she said, reaching for a cookie.

The man took one for himself and then a sly grin crossed over his lips. "Don't tell my wife about this if you see her around, or she might not let me have a piece of her apple pie when we get home."

"Your secret is safe with me, especially because I have no idea who your wife is."

The man pointed to a woman bent over a rose bush across the yard with her nose pressed into a flower bloom. "That's my Martha, and I'm John."

"As in the Bennetts? You own the Sea Turtle Inn."

"That's us. Do you remember delivering lobsters to our inn with your dad when you were just a wee one?"

"Sort of, but mostly I recall playing the grand piano in the entryway of the inn."

"Yup, and when it was time to leave, but you

wanted to play Twinkle Twinkle Little Star over and over again, Henry sat on the bench and waited until it was your choice to go."

"He was the best parent I could ever ask for, but I wish that I had the opportunity to acknowledge it to him, one more time."

"Henry was a good man to everyone. Without him, our business might not have survived all these years."

"How so?"

"There were seasons over the years when the price of lobster was too high for us to purchase it. Our customers count on their lobster dinner included with their night's stay. It's what sets us apart from all the other bed and breakfasts in the area. Henry sold to us at reduced prices, even when it wasn't profitable for him, just so that we could stay in business."

"I was told earlier today that Laurel Cove was like a big family." Willa left out the *dysfunctional* term that Brynn had used. "That must have been what my father believed too, and that's why he did what he could to help."

"Well, whatever his reason was, he will surely be missed by many."

John reached for another cookie but his hand was slapped away before it got to the plate. Martha shook her finger at him. "Don't you dare touch those treats. Are the insulin shots not enough of a punishment for your overeating?"

John's face turned red and he slunk down in his seat.

Willa pulled the plate closer to herself. "It's my fault; I've been eating these nonstop since I got here and I asked John to take them away from me. He was just taking one to be polite."

Martha looked at him from the corner of her eye and then patted down his wind-blown hair on the back of his head. "My husband can be quite the gentleman when he wants to be," she glared at him playfully, "especially if it involves breaking his diet."

"He's very excited about the apple pie you baked for him tonight; please don't let my mistake cost him his dessert."

"I suppose a little slice won't do him too much harm." Martha leaned in close to Willa's ear and whispered, "Just between you and me, I've cut the sugar in the recipe in half over the years, but he hasn't caught on yet."

Willa winked at her. "My lips are sealed."

Martha took off over the embankment, spreading her fingertips out to her sides, and letting them touch the tops of the purple and white lupins covering the ground.

"You seem to have inherited the honor that your father had in him."

Willa's cheeks flushed. "I wouldn't call that honor."

"You haven't witnessed my wife huffing at me from behind her newspaper all night." John stood up to follow Martha. "There are times when doing something small can make a big difference in someone's life." Willa watched as John approached Martha and wrapped an arm around her waist. He plucked a bloom from one of the flowers and tucked it behind her ear before planting a kiss on her cheek. Willa let out a contented sigh and rested her chin between the palms of her hands as she continued to watch the elderly couple frolic in the flowers like young lovers. Even the sound of the chair pulling out next to her didn't fully pull her attention away from them.

Beth smiled at Willa, who looked to be in a peaceful state. "I see you've been talking to some of your father's friends."

Willa nodded. "They spoke very highly of him," she said while keeping her focus on the loving couple.

Beth caught sight of what Willa was enthralled with. "They are quite fortunate to still have each other after all these years."

"When I was young, I only wanted Dad all to myself, but after I left home, I wished that he would find a woman that he could settle down with."

"I asked Henry about that once. He said that the love he shared with your mother was enough for an entire lifetime for him and that there wasn't room in his heart for another."

Willa closed her eyes and tried to bring up the image in her mind of her parents together, from photographs that she had seen. "That's the kind of love that I hope I'll have someday."

"You and me both, dear."

A slight grin spread across Willa's lips. "I noticed that your librarian friend showed up to support you today."

Beth crossed her fingers together as if they were holding a secret within them. "Indeed, he did."

"So, my next visit to Maine might involve a happier event, perhaps a wedding?"

"There will be *no* such thing." Beth stood and made a show of starting to walk away, but as she passed by Willa, she leaned in to add, "One must have a proper engagement prior to making wedding plans."

Willa spun on her chair to face Beth, her eyes lit

up with excitement. "It's about time our family grows a little bigger."

"Then maybe you'll add to it too by starting to work on a family of your own."

"I doubt there's anyone out there that would be willing to put up with my crazy lifestyle."

"Oh hush, if I was able to find a soulmate at my ripe old age, then a successful, beautiful woman such as yourself will have no problem at all. Heck, I've already seen someone pining after you in the short time you've been here. Now, give me a hug so I get back before it's too dark to see the road."

Willa stood and was pulled into one of her aunt's tight embraces. "*Pining?* Who are you talking about?"

"It's not for me to tell; open your eyes and you'll figure it out soon enough."

Beth pinched her cheek as if she was five years old again and took off with a bounce in her step. Willa watched her disappear around the corner of the house, sifting through her mind as to who could possibly be interested in her to the point that her aunt was able to pick up on it, at a funeral of all places. It was then that she remembered both Shannon and Megan had come to sit on either side of her during the service. It must have looked to her aunt that either one of them might have feelings for her beyond friendship, especially with Shannon offering up her home for the gathering. Willa smiled warmly to herself, knowing that she would never find better friends than the two of them.

The night wore on and as the food started to vanish, so did the guests, until only Shannon and Willa remained. "Will you please just put those in the dishwasher and stop doing them all by hand?" Shannon insisted, reaching for the spoon in Willa's hand.

Willa pulled the spoon out of Shannon's reach. "I can have these all washed, dried, and put away before that thing can finish a wash cycle," she said, scooping up a frothy bundle of soap suds from the sink and dabbing them on the tip of Shannon's nose.

Shannon wiped away the bubbles with a dishcloth. "Fine, but at least let me help you dry them." She pulled up a stool to the counter and started in on the pile of dishes that Willa had stacked next to the sink.

"Did you get some opportunities to connect with anyone in the midst of being a hostess?" Willa asked.

"I did here and there, although just about every conversation began with a health update."

"Ugh, seriously?"

"I literally had to stop Mr. Stockton from pulling his pants down in the middle of the dining room to show me the hives on his thighs."

"People have no shame, or dignity for that matter, do they?"

"Either that or they just want to save money by not having to pay the office fee for the diagnosis."

"I completely understand what it's like to question the intentions of everyone around you, but at least you can count on the genuine friendship from Meg and me."

"And if you hadn't returned to Laurel Cove, who knows if the three of us would have found each other."

Willa acknowledged that she owed her newfound friends to her father's passing. She set aside the dish she was rinsing, picked up the two filled wine glasses from the counter, and handed one to Shannon. She raised her own into the air. "To Dad, for bringing us together."

Shannon raised her glass to Willa's. "To Henry."

Chapter Eighteen

Willa groaned as she started to wake and flopped an arm over her eyes to block out the bright rays of sunlight pouring through the windows. She turned towards the back of the couch to hide even more of her face, but when she did, she found that something was very off about her sleeping situation. She had become accustomed to waking up on her father's couch lately, after dealing with restless nights, but unlike the soft old leather she was used to feeling surrounding her, she was now on a fluffy cushion covered in a layer of velvet material.

She fought through the pain of opening her eyes while adjusting to the brightness of the room and recognized immediately that she was still in Shannon's house. A pillow, which was not one of the decorative ones meant just for show, was placed under her head, and a quilt was tucked around her body. Willa sat up and swallowed down the dryness in her throat. She felt slightly queasy and she clutched at the insistent pounding at the base of her head.

A note left on the side table caught her eye, which read: *Drink all of the water and take both of the pills. One is for your headache and the other for nausea. Please lock up if you leave.* Behind the piece of paper was a plate with a muffin and two tiny pills on it. Next to it was a tall glass of water.

Willa tried to think back to the previous night

and what had led to her not leaving Shannon's house, but her mind was too fuzzy to find the answers she was searching for. It wasn't until she brought the water glass and plate to the kitchen when she noticed the two empty bottles of wine on the counter. There was no way that Shannon would have drank much more than a glass or two before working the following morning, which meant that she had to have consumed the rest of it on her own.

"Ugh, no wonder I can't remember anything," she complained out loud to herself.

Willa cleaned up any remnants left of last night's gathering and from her unexpected stay. On her way out the door, she found her purse, keys, and glasses, which were folded neatly, on the entryway table. Her heels were placed on the floor below it. She figured that Shannon must have removed her glasses and shoes for her, because she would never have placed them in such an orderly fashion in her state last night.

The time display on her car dashboard showed that it was after two already. She rubbed her eyes and checked it again before referring to her cell phone to confirm its authenticity. She let out a sigh of relief that she wasn't still crashed out on the couch when Shannon got back from work.

With no particular plans set for the day, other than attempting to pack up her father's house, she took a leisurely drive around the island. When she approached the Mussels by the Sea sign, she recalled Brynn saying that Griffin would be gone by the afternoon. She slowed her car and decided to pull into the parking lot, but not before double and triple checking that his truck was nowhere to be seen.

The gym was busier than the last time she

was there, with quite a few people using the cardio equipment as well as in the weight lifting section, but Brynn wasn't in either of those areas. Willa realized that she must have looked out of place as she wandered around the outskirts of the room because a burly young man in a sweat covered T-shirt pointed to the doublewide doors in the back that led to the indoor courts.

"The owner is through there if you need her," he grunted as he continued to use his dumbbell weights. Willa decided that she liked that the younger generation on the island either didn't know who she was, or that they just didn't care.

She made her way to the other section of the gym and followed the distinct sound of rubber soles and wheels squealing against the basketball court floors. When she came into view of Brynn taking a shot at the hoop on the opposite wall from her, she leaned against the row of bleachers to watch her. What she didn't pay attention to was that Brynn's opponent, Cassidy, saw her come in and was now taking long strides in her direction. Before Willa had time to back away, she was up in her face.

"I thought I told you to keep your distance from Brynn," Cassidy whispered through gritted teeth. She glanced over her shoulder to make sure that Brynn wasn't watching.

"I don't know what your problem is with me, but I'm pretty sure Brynn wants to talk to me."

"Regardless of what she wants, you being here for a short while and then leaving again will only hurt her more. The only way she'll heal is if you stay away for good."

"In case you haven't noticed after twenty years,

her injury is permanent."

"I wasn't referring to her physical injury."

Willa started to process what Cassidy meant, but Brynn finally noticed them and interrupted their conversation.

"Cass, you're not being rude to my guest, are you?"

"Nope, just heading to the shower." Cassidy stormed away with heavy footsteps and let the door slam shut behind her.

"Sorry about that. She can be a little intense sometimes."

Cassidy was more intimidating and threatening to her than just intense, but there was no way that she would admit that to Brynn. Willa couldn't help but wonder again if there was something more between them than friendship, which made her angry that Cassidy was making out with another woman in the bathroom at the reunion. She had to try and find out exactly what their relationship was before she accused Cassidy of cheating.

"She's clearly very protective of you. It's good to see that you've remained *friends* after all these years." Willa hinted at wanting to know just how close of friends they were.

"Everyone who stays in Laurel Cove is friends with one another. The smaller the community, the tighter the bond."

Even though Brynn's comment wasn't aimed at insulting Willa, she felt a pang of hurt jolt through her. She had voluntarily given up her right to years of friendship because she had chosen to run from the problems that she believed she had created. "I'm glad that you're surrounded by a good support system of people."

"I lost one of the best this week," Brynn paused as she smoothed out the anguish forming on her face, "but it brought you back into my life, so something good came of it."

The words that Cassidy had said moments earlier repeated themselves in Willa's mind and she questioned what she was doing that was so wrong. Then another voice entered her mind and she flashed back to when Griffin yelled at her in the hospital waiting room, telling her that Brynn didn't want to see her. "Now that the funeral is over with, if you don't want to see me, I'll understand."

"Geez, Willa, I wasn't pretending to be nice to you just because your dad died."

Willa pulled off her glasses, squeezed her eyes shut and pinched at the bridge of her nose before replacing her glasses. "I promise I wasn't purposely accusing you of something so horrendous. It's my own insecurities ruining everything again."

"Hey, don't be so hard on yourself. We share a unique history together and it makes sense that you'd be apprehensive about it, but I want you to trust me when I tell you that *we're* going to be okay."

"It may take some time for me to get used to that concept, but will you stick with me through the process?"

"Of course. I'll always be here for you." Brynn's smile spread across her face. "Speaking of which, are you here to take me up on the offer of making plans to do something together?"

Willa ran a hand through her hair and awkwardly shifted her weight from one leg to the other. "Uh, yeah, I know you're probably busy working, but I was thinking that because Griff will be gone for a while, maybe you could use some help around here."

"I did give him a list of things that I needed him to do before he left and of course he slacked off and got nothing done, so if you'd be willing, I'd appreciate the help."

Willa's face lit up with a wide smile and she opened her arms out. "What would you like me to start with first?"

Brynn chuckled. "Right now, I think it's best if you go back to the house."

"Are you sure there's nothing I can help with now?"

"Willa," Brynn took her hand and spoke softly even though no one was in earshot, "you're still wearing the clothes you had on at the funeral."

She looked down at the severely wrinkled black pants suit that she was still dressed in, and was embarrassed that she had forgotten to clean herself up before her impromptu visit to the gym. "I fell asleep on Shannon's couch last night." She didn't want to admit to Brynn that she had become so inebriated that she couldn't leave even if she wanted to.

"I'm glad you stayed. It worried me that you might be alone last night."

Willa wondered then if Shannon thought the same way and encouraged her to drink enough to make sure that she would have no choice but to stay. It also allowed her to have a full night's sleep, which she would have had difficulty with alone, with her father's remains looming above on the mantle. "She has been so supportive throughout this week for me. I have no idea how to repay her for the kindness."

"She doesn't expect anything in return. Shannon

is a natural nurturer and that's why she makes a great doctor and an even better friend."

"You're right; I have to get used to a place where people do things for each other for no other agenda than because they care."

"You also need to begin showing a little care for yourself. Go get cleaned up and relax for a while. Meet me back here this evening and allow me to take you out for dinner."

"That sounds lovely, but how did this go from me giving you a hand, to you buying me dinner?"

"There are a couple of things that I need help with tonight when I close up. That is, if you're willing to come back here with me after we finish eating?"

"I would be delighted to have a meal with you, and to offer as much help as you need."

Chapter Nineteen

Willa stood in the driveway, staring into the trunk of her tiny sports car. Griffin had made a comment about how Brynn's wheelchair would never fit in it, and now she could see that he might be right about that. She tried to picture the dimensions of the wheels and how long the seat was in comparison to the depth of her trunk, but the compartment space seemed too small. She climbed into the driver's seat and looked to the back of her car, but because there were only two doors and barely enough space for passengers to squeeze back there, she didn't think that the chair would fit there either.

Her open hand came up and she slapped the top of her steering wheel with enough force to need to rub the pain away from the palm afterwards. She cursed the fact that if she were in the city right now, it would be so simple to get a car and a driver at her door within minutes, but she hadn't thought about transportation until the last minute when she remembered that Brynn wanted to go *out* for dinner. A glance at the clock on her dash showed that there wasn't much time, but she might be able to pick up ingredients at the grocery store, and possibly fumble her way through cooking a meal at Brynn's house. A sigh of frustration escaped from her just as the answer to her problems came into view, as she looked up at the garage door.

She moved her tiny car over to the other side of

the driveway and went back into the house to get her father's truck keys. As she opened the door leading to the garage from the house, another wave of memories flooded her. An antique rocking chair in the corner of the room, with well-worn armrests, was her father's favorite location to repair lobster traps and paint buoys. If she ever needed to find him, he was sure to be hard at work in this spot, with either a length of rope or a brush in his hand.

Willa made her way over to the truck and gripped the metal handle. Opening the door came at the risk of opening the floodgates of her emotions, but she willed the strength to keep it together. She pulled herself up into the seat and the door creaked shut, showing the age of the rusty hinges. The old pickup was the first and only vehicle that her father had ever owned in his lifetime and it was already well past its prime when he bought it. It wasn't that he couldn't afford a new one; it was that he didn't see the point in getting rid of something as long as it could be fixed. Willa shook her head at how many times that old truck had to be repaired over the years.

When she started earning a high enough income from adapting the screenplay versions of her books to films, her Father's Day gift to her dad was an unlimited account at the local garage to keep his truck running. The locals may have been believing that she was frivolous by spending unheard of amounts of money on her sports car, but if they only knew how much went into rebuilt engines, replaced axels, rust repair, and the countless other expenses to keep that old truck legally registered, they wouldn't judge her so harshly.

Willa turned the key in the ignition and closed her eyes for a moment, recalling the way it felt the first day she learned to drive in that very seat at sixteen years old. The memories continued to come to her the entire ride to Brynn's house as she was reminded of first dates, camping trips, drive-in movies, and being dropped off at elementary school every morning for years. There was no possible way that she could sell this truck, even if it meant that she had to have it stored somewhere in the city.

"Griff isn't here," Willa repeated to herself on the way up the walkway to Brynn's house, and yet her stomach shook nervously. She raised her hand to knock, but the door opened before her knuckles met the wood.

"Damn, you sure did change your sense of style after Hollywood got a hold of you." A glimmer of admiration shone in Brynn's eyes as she marveled at the simple, yet elegant black cocktail dress that Willa wore.

Willa blushed, so she quickly diverted the attention back on Brynn. "I'd say you made the more drastic change." She leaned down and straightened the collar of Brynn's button up dress shirt. "I can't remember a time when you wore anything other than a jersey for whatever sport you playing for the season."

"Hey, it was my duty as team captain to show my school spirit by representing the sport."

"Your mom confessed to me once that you hated doing laundry so much that you wore your uniform just to have less clothes to wash."

Brynn raised her hands up in surrender. "Guilty and I admit to still hating to do laundry."

"Don't worry; we all detest it."

Brynn checked her watch. "We should get going. I have reservations for us." She motioned for Willa to start down the ramp in front of her.

Willa hesitated, feeling as though she should let Brynn go ahead of her. She stepped aside awkwardly and pushed herself against the porch railing to leave enough room for Brynn to get by.

Brynn rolled her eyes and smirked. "Go on. I promise I won't ram into your ankles," she insisted. Willa did as she was told and proceeded down the wooden ramp as swiftly as her heels and the opening of her form fitted dress would allow. She could tell by the sound of the wheelchair breaking behind her that Brynn could have gone much faster without her in front, but even as children, she had always treated Willa with a chivalrous respect.

"Oh, you got the truck out on the road, huh?" Brynn observed as they rounded the corner to the driveway.

"I figured it would be better than my car because of what Griff said yesterday."

"Don't pay attention to him. He was just being a jerk. My chair disassembles into smaller pieces."

"Well, it's okay because it will fit fine in the bed of the truck."

"You do realize I can't get up into that seat?"

"Oh," Willa paused, trying to figure out the situation, "but you ride in Griff's truck?"

"He lifts me into the seat. I doubt you can heft me up there, especially in that skin-tight dress."

Willa's heart sank. She had allowed herself to be bullied into believing something that wasn't even true. She considered going back to switch out the truck for her car, but she was concerned about the timeframe for the reservation. Her fingers tightened around the tiny sequined clutch purse in her hand, as she fought an internal struggle with herself to figure out a solution.

"Since I was the one who offered to take you out for dinner, do you mind if we take my car?"

Willa's head tilted and her eyes narrowed. "Of course. I didn't know that you..." She trailed off, not wanting to imply that Brynn wasn't capable of driving, though she couldn't understand how.

Brynn pressed a button on her keychain and the garage door raised up to reveal an all-wheel drive car. "Hand controls, if you hadn't figured it out yet."

"Ah, right." Willa took ownership of her ignorance with a nod.

Fascinated, she observed the entire process from the open passenger door, as Brynn slid inside, broke down her wheelchair, and packed the pieces into the back seat. Then she got in and sat back, to take in the experience of learning the control system of having an accelerator and brake on a pole that extended up from the floor of the car.

"You can try driving it sometime if you want," Brynn offered as she backed the car out onto the street.

"Knowing me, I'd probably panic and do something wrong."

Brynn laughed. "The pedals are still down there if you need them."

"Hmm, that's good to know, but it would be safer for both of us if I just watch."

"Your style may have changed, but your personality hasn't."

"What makes you say that?"

"You've always been eager to learn new things, but too timid to try them out."

Willa turned to look at Brynn with her mouth dropped open wide in a show of sarcastic insult, but then folded her arms across her chest and pouted her surrender. "You're right. The only risks I take are the fake ones that I put my characters through in my stories."

"Don't be so hard on yourself. It's not a bad trait, and it can be easily remedied if you're up to the challenge. Maybe we could go on a couple of adventures this week, if you've got the time?"

"I suppose," Willa flashed her a warning glare, "but it better not be anything to do with jumping out of an airplane." She pointed a finger in Brynn's direction so that she would know how serious her threat was.

Brynn chuckled. "I promise that I wouldn't expect you to do something that I can't, and in case you haven't noticed, I'm not very skilled at jumping."

Willa shifted so that she leaned her elbow on the armrest molded into the car door. Even though her eyes followed the scenery along the side of the road that they passed by, she was completely disinterested in the view.

"Everything okay over there?" Brynn asked. "You got really quiet All of sudden."

Willa sighed and redirected her attention back to Brynn. "You may have had the last twenty years to get used to your situation, but to me, it's still new. When you make jokes about yourself, I can't help but feel like the jab is aimed at me for putting you in that position."

"You're not the only one to feel that way. I've had this conversation with just about everyone in my life at some point. The thing is, I *need* to stay lighthearted about being the way I am, or else reality sets in, and I get down."

Willa reached across the center console and rested the back of her hand against Brynn's side. "I'm sorry. I was only thinking of my own feelings and not how it affected you."

"Let's make a deal. In the future, I'll try to make a conscious effort to keep the wisecracks about my disability to a minimum, but I would also like for you to try to be open-minded about potentially making some jokes about it yourself."

Willa stared back at Brynn with raised eyebrows. "I don't know about that."

"It might be good for you to help alleviate the guilt you think you have. They say that laughter is the best medicine, after all." Brynn took the opportunity at a stop sign to offer Willa one of her genuine grins that made any sort of misunderstanding between them fade away.

"Oh, all right, but I'm not going to force something. It has to come to me naturally, or else it's not going to happen."

Chapter Twenty

Willa had become so engaged in conversation with Brynn that she hadn't noticed that they had crossed the bridge over to the mainland until they reached the downtown section of the bustling community. "Oh, I didn't know we were coming all the way out here for dinner."

"What did you expect? That I would take you to The Anchor to eat?"

"Possibly." Willa let the word fall slowly out of her mouth.

"I can't believe you would assume that I lacked enough class to take you somewhere extravagant."

"Hmm, well, the last time you took me out, it was for a hotdog and popcorn, but I suppose I could let that slide since it was the best that money could buy at a high school concession stand."

"If I didn't need two hands to drive this car, I'd reach over and backhand your shoulder right now." Brynn flashed her a playful grin.

"Good to know. Remind me in the future to always have disagreements with you while you're behind the wheel."

The streets were swarming with summer tourists visiting the area, and musical performances at the college in town brought even more people than usual to the business district. Brynn slowed the car down and scanned the area.

"There's no way you're going to find parking on this street this time of evening." Just as the words came out of Willa's mouth, Brynn pulled into a spot in the very front of the restaurant. When Willa looked at her with amazement, Brynn pointed to the sign above the parking spot. Willa arched her head to get a better look and then caught sight of the blue sign with the wheelchair symbol on it.

"Guaranteed parking is the best perk out of them all."

"That would come in really handy in New York."

"Maybe I could go down and visit you someday. If you wanted, that is."

"I'd like that a lot, actually."

Brynn smiled and motioned to the backseat. "I need you to get out first so that I don't whack you in the head while taking my wheels out of the car."

"Oh, right," Willa said. She started to open her door when she noticed the amount of people passing by on the sidewalk. She paused briefly to pull down the visor and expose the mirror behind it. She checked the state of her makeup and readjusted her hair over her shoulders.

"Now this is definitely a new side of you that I haven't seen before."

"If I had known ahead of time that we were leaving the island, I would have prepared you for what we might have to deal with, if my fans notice me out there. It could mean random photos and autographs, just to warn you." Willa exited the car and made her way over to Brynn's open door to give her the space to get out, while still being able to talk.

"I can handle that, but I did book a private room for us to dine in, so you won't have to worry about being interrupted by anyone while we eat."

"Private?"

"Yeah, I hope you're open to unique dining experiences."

"It sounds intriguing, but it's the privacy that I'm looking forward to."

When Willa heard private, she assumed that Brynn scored one of the more secluded booths in the back corner of the restaurant, but they soon passed by all of those tables that were already filled with other guests. As they were ushered through a door next to the kitchen entrance, Willa remembered that there was a large room available to rent for parties or other events with a group of people too big for the regular dining area.

They had both been in there once for a classmate's middle school birthday party. The one memory Willa had from that day was that the girl's mother insisted that they all wear pink princess birthday hats. Brynn was angry and pouted the whole time, so Willa gave her the frosting off her slice of cake to cheer her up. She turned back to glance at Brynn, and it occurred to her that she would offer up her entire dessert to keep that smile on her face, even if just for a fleeting moment.

They approached the event room and Willa hoped that Brynn didn't pay for the enormous space, for the sake of avoiding the recognition of random strangers. While she would appreciate the solitude, it would feel strange sitting at a table meant for a couple of dozen people. Her concerns were laid to rest, though, when they turned and entered a small room no larger than a walk-in closet. The hostess closed the door behind them and Willa looked between her and Brynn for the answer as to why they were confined in a tiny empty space together.

The hostess excused herself and slipped between Willa and Brynn to disappear behind a black silk curtain that was the same color as the black walls, making it blend in to the point of being invisible. "Come right in," the hostess urged them to enter. Willa followed, knowing that Brynn would make her go first anyway, and she held the satin fabric aside so that Brynn's wheels wouldn't get caught on the bottom of it.

Inside was a space just large enough to hold a table for two. One of the chairs was already removed to accommodate a space for Brynn to pull right up to the table. The only light source in the dimly lit room was from a single candle in the center of the table. Willa realized as she observed her surroundings that what contributed to the dimness was that the walls were painted black as well as the table cloth, table settings and furnishings. This was all such a stark contrast to the bright colors used throughout the rest of the restaurant.

The hostess removed an odd-looking contraption from a shelf on the wall behind her and placed it on her head. Willa gasped and leaned away from her when the woman pulled the goggles down over her eyes. The woman lifted the bottom of her goggles up at Willa's reaction to the strange device. "Usually people inform their dinner date of what is about to happen, but I guess she'll fill you in with the details after we begin." The goggles were then replaced, and Willa raised a questioning eyebrow at the mysterious dinner experience that she was about to embark on. Across the table, Brynn winked at her and grinned, before the hostess bent down and blew out the candle.

Shrouded in complete darkness, Willa sat frozen

and wide eyed as she heard the sound of the woman walk away and close the door behind her. She blinked a few times, unable to tell if her eyes were open or closed in the blackness.

At home, while she slept with the lights out, there was always light coming from random sources. Chargers for the cellphone and laptop, neon signs from businesses nearby, and the consistent flow of traffic on the street below, kept some sort of glow no matter how soft, peeking through the darkness. Here, though, there was nothing visible, even after the typical adjustment period that eyes need to go through when the lights are first shut off. The dead silence also made it eerie, until the familiar deep chuckle that emanated only from Brynn broke through and lit up the room with sound.

"Have you ever done dinner in the dark before?"

"No, but some of the trendy restaurants in New York are offering it. I would have given it a try if I had someone to go with."

"I'm glad I picked something that wouldn't completely scare you away."

"This could be fun, now that I know those were night vision goggles, and I'm not about to become a victim in some steampunk horror flick."

"Ha, yes, it is scary the first time you see them on the waitress, especially when you know that they can see you, but you can't see them."

"First time. So you've been here before?"

"Just once, but I was by myself the last time."

"This seems like a peculiar thing to do on your own." The words came out of Willa's mouth even though she meant to keep them within the confines of her own mind. She supposed that the darkness might have some sort of effect on her openness, which she would have to work to suppress before she blurted out all of her thoughts.

"There was no one available to go with me at the time and it was suggested that I do it as part of my therapy."

Willa giggled. "Since when does stuffing your face with no lights on help out with your physical therapy?"

Brynn was quiet for a long time, so long that Willa almost called out her name to be sure that she was still there.

"Not *that* kind of therapy."

Willa closed her eyes, although it was still pitch dark, and took in as deep a breath as she could, as silently as possible. "It was my one hope over the years that you wouldn't need to see someone because of what happened."

"It's ironic that I worried about the same thing for you."

"Well, it seems as though both of our fears have come true." Willa sighed. "Although, it sounds like your therapist has some more entertaining methods for treatment than mine does. Would it be overstepping any boundaries to ask what you are supposed to get out of this?"

"Nah, I don't mind sharing. I think that she wanted me to spend some time with a different disability other than my own, so that I would have a greater appreciation for what I do have going for me."

"And did you find it helpful?"

"Actually, I got more out of it than I expected."

"How so?"

"Not being able to see my meal made me rely on other senses such as taste and smell to enjoy it. I found that everything was better in a different sort of way, such as the flavors standing out more to me. I related this concept to my injury and how I used to really love soccer and softball, but now I've found a love for basketball and tennis. I would have never focused on those sports before, and now it might get me into the Paralympics someday."

A slight weight was lifted from Willa's heart when she learned that Brynn could still pursue her love of sports. The darkness made her wonder how she would be able to continue writing if she were to lose her sight. She shuddered to think about having to rely on voice activated computer programs that would hinder her personal creative process.

"Please tell me that you're not going to ever say that what happened to you was a blessing in disguise," Willa pleaded.

"Hell no, those words will never come out of my mouth."

The waitress dropped off an array of wine tastings for Willa and beers for Brynn. Fortunately, they were lined up on a wooden tray with a carved surface to hold the glasses in place as they fumbled about in a search for each little glass. When Willa inquired how they were going to see a menu to order, she was informed that they were going to be served a predetermined seven-course meal of tiny plates, because the best way to experience the meal was to not know what they were putting into their mouths until they tasted it.

The first couple of courses were appetizers that were served so that each bite was already set up on a separate spoon, making it a simple process to find on the table. Willa successfully found the correct end of the spoon, but as she lifted it to her face, she misjudged where it should have gone into her mouth, and it instead bounced off the corner of her lip, hitting her cheek. Most of the contents of the spoonful landed on her lap.

"I'm glad of two things tonight: that these napkins are thick and that I chose to wear black." Willa laughed. "Oh, and also that you can't see me laughing with my mouth stuffed full of food."

"I know what you mean; my shirt soaked up more beer than my mouth did."

"Mmm...I have no idea what I'm eating right now, but it tastes delightful."

"Is it that soft stuff with the crunchy crumble on top?"

"Yes, like sweet potato with a spicy kick to it."

"Yeah, I'm guilty of licking the plate at this very moment because I can't figure out where it landed when it fell off my spoon."

Willa tried to suppress her laughter by holding a hand over her mouth to keep from spitting out her sip of wine. "If the woman with the night vision goggles were in here now, I'd pay her good money to let me borrow them for a minute to watch you do that."

"Hmm, well, if you do that, then I'd alert the media to where you're eating dinner. Imagine the headlines with photos of you with a wet spot on the front of your dress and food stuck to the front of your chest."

"I'd tell them that I didn't want my date, who can't feed herself, to feel embarrassed, and so I dropped food all over myself to match her."

"So, you consider this a *date*, huh?"

Willa stopped chewing the bite of food she had taken and swallowed it down in one large gulp. "I didn't necessarily mean *that* kind of date," she stammered out uneasily.

"Willa, I'm just messing with you," she said in such a calm voice that Willa had a difficult time discerning if it was Brynn's way of avoiding serious situations, as she was known for doing.

Willa decided to take advantage of this opening to inquire about her involvement with Cassidy. "I doubt your watchdog, Cassidy, would appreciate me taking you out on a date."

"She's more bark than bite and she can't control who I spend my time with."

"So you're not together?"

"A long time ago we were, but we work better together as training partners than we did as a couple." Willa tried to place how she could simultaneously have sadness for her friend's loss of a relationship and yet be pleased that Brynn didn't end up with someone as rude as Cassidy seemed to be.

"I'm glad she's an ex because I didn't know how to break it to you that I caught her in the school restroom making out with some woman. Cass looked like she was trying to hide what she was doing, so I figured she was cheating."

"It's the other way around, actually. Cass is a gym teacher and the other woman teaches math. She's a married woman and they're trying to keep their affair a secret until her divorce is final."

"Ah, that explains the sneaking around."

"I can ask her to tone down on the verbal attacks if she's still being uncivil to you."

"No, please don't. I need to be the one to mend any animosities that people still have towards me. The same goes for Griff."

"That's understandable. I'll stay out of it."

The multiple small plates of food added up to way too much than Willa had been used to consuming and by the time the dessert platter was brought out, she offered it all to Brynn.

"Okay, but you're missing out. This place has the best desserts in town." Brynn described in detail how scrumptious every tiny dessert item was as she ate it, from tarts and pies to chocolate mousse cups and miniature cookies. The sounds of delight coming from Brynn made Willa crave for just one piece of the sweets that she knew were located somewhere on the table in front of her. She reached out to find a tiny soft square on the platter and took a bite of it.

"Oh my, it's your favorite, carrot cake."

"What! I haven't come across that yet."

"Lean your head across the table towards me as far as you can go."

Willa reached out her empty hand until she could feel Brynn's jawline. She followed it down until she cupped her chin in her fingertips, then she stretched out the hand with the carrot cake in it until it touched her lips. She could feel Brynn's mouth open and she nudged the piece in between her open lips.

"Mmm, it's absolutely heavenly."

When Willa went to pull away from her face, Brynn clasped her hand around Willa's wrist to hold it there. Willa felt the soft, wet warmth of Brynn's lips as she sucked off the cake frosting smeared on her fingertips. When Brynn released her wrist, Willa slowly pulled her finger back out of Brynn's mouth, although her lips kept a firm suction on it until the end of her finger came out, and then Brynn left a soft kiss on the tip of it.

Willa's body buzzed with a wild energy she fought to contain in the darkness.

When they had been teenagers, Brynn always exuded a playful teasing towards Willa. It was like a game between twins to see who could make Willa squirm in a flustered state with the comments that they could come up with. While it was all in fun, Brynn respected the fact that Griffin and Willa were a couple and that she was only the best friend. Willa had never even considered the idea that Brynn had really wanted to be anything more to her until she professed her feelings to her on their graduation night. The night that she responded by causing permanent damage to Brynn's body. The thought of that night brought the memories flooding back to Willa and a terrorizing fear replaced her excited tingle.

Willa left an agonizingly long silence lingering between them and Brynn had to have noticed it too. "Did I cross a line that I shouldn't have? I can't see your face to know if what I did was wrong."

Willa wanted to keep things simple and lighthearted between them tonight. She yearned to blurt out that everything was fine and make some sort of comment about Brynn missing a patch of frosting on one of her fingers. She wanted to forget about everything else in their past and relish the sensation still lingering from Brynn's mouth surrounding her finger. What had stopped her from fulfilling her desires was that the darkness provided enough security that she had the courage to truthfully expose her innermost fear. "After you kissed me, I hurt you and I don't remember why I did it. I'm afraid that it could happen again."

"Willa…"

Willa could hear Brynn's hand carefully searching the area in front of her, but only grazing upon silverware, plates, and glasses because she had withdrawn her hand into her lap. She didn't feel worthy of the compassion that Brynn was sure to show her. The rustling sounds soon stopped and Willa guessed that Brynn must have given up on trying for a physical connection between them.

"If I had a way with words like you do, I'd like to think that I would have expressed how I felt about you, without doing something as crazy as kissing you in front of your boyfriend, my brother. Your response was well deserved for the disrespect I showed you."

"For twenty years, my mind has replayed what I can remember of that night over and over again. The one part that I know for sure is that when you kissed me, I didn't want it to end."

"You didn't?"

"No, I know without a doubt that I wasn't upset with you for what happened. That's what makes my reaction to it so unsettling for me." Willa waited for Brynn to respond, but this time, she was the reserved one. "You have reason to be angry with me now that you know there was absolutely no rationality behind my backlash," Willa said, gripping the seat of her chair as she waited for a response.

"Please don't misinterpret my silence as anger. I spent the last two decades thinking that I inappropriately took advantage of my best friend. I'm just relieved that I didn't."

The sound of the waitress coming back into the room paused their conversation briefly as she lit a tea candle and placed it in the center of the table. "This will get you acclimated to the light again before I come back to bring you out. I hope you had a wonderful dining experience with us this evening."

Brynn and Willa both nodded through squinted eyelids before they found themselves alone again. A scattered mess of crumbs, splattered food, and spilled liquid from the drinks covered the table. Willa shook off her napkin from her lap and wiped off her chin for any remnants of food still stuck on it. She forced herself to look into Brynn's eyes, finding that the truth of the matter was so much more difficult to say aloud when she was faced with the object of her greatest fear and desire rolled into one. "The chaos of what's left of our dinner is representative of our discussion, isn't it?"

"I think the lesson we both learned from tonight's conversation is that if we had just talked to each other after the incident, then we could have saved many years' worth of self-blame on ourselves as well as lots of therapy bills."

"I agree. If there is to be any chance of us to have a friendship like we did before, then I need to know that you won't shut me out again."

"Shut you out? Willa, you left me when I needed you the most."

Willa's heart pounded in her chest and a wave of nausea passed through her. The room became all too small for her, with the single flickering flame seeming to expose her in ways that a bright fluorescent light could never do.

"I slept in the hospital waiting room every night for a week. Griff came out and told me that I should leave, because you never wanted to see me again," Willa said in a voice so low that it could barely be considered a whisper.

Brynn's face flushed even through her dark skin

and her eyes glazed over as she released her glass of water and balled her hand up into a fist. "*You* were the person I asked for when I came out of my first surgery. I *begged* Griff and Mom to bring you to me. He told me that you never came and then I gave up when I heard that you had left the state."

Willa placed her hand on her chest, over her heart. She wanted to hold it in place, because it felt to her as though it was sinking. There had to be a reasonable excuse for Griffin's behavior. "He was hurt."

"*I* was hurt. He fucking lied to me and you."

Chapter Twenty-one

Willa stood on the sidewalk and winced every time Brynn removed a section of her wheelchair and tossed each piece with much more force than was needed into the backseat of the car. When she was sure that there was no chance of being whacked in the head by a flying piece of metal, she got in and wrapped her hands around Brynn's arm in an attempt to calm her. Willa opened her mouth to offer some words to help ease her rage, but became momentarily preoccupied by the hefty bicep muscle beneath her palms.

Brynn backed out of the parking spot and roughly pushed down on her pedal extender, causing the car to jerk and accelerate faster than normal. "I need to get to the fitness center to beat the hell out of a punching bag. I'll drop you off at your truck first, though."

"Oh, no, you won't. The deal was dinner in exchange for helping you out at the gym and I intend on fulfilling my end of the bargain, especially since you sneakily prepaid for dinner when you made the reservation."

"And what exactly do you think you'll accomplish for work, wearing that?" Brynn raised her eyebrows and glanced at Willa's form fitted dress and high heels.

"Hey, don't underestimate the ability of a woman in a cocktail dress."

A half an hour later, Willa cursed to herself as she reached out from the top of a ladder to remove the heavily frayed net from a basketball hoop so that she could replace it with a new one.

"Are you regretting the decision to turn down the offer to borrow a pair of sweatpants yet?" Brynn asked from the base of the ladder.

"The ones you pulled out of the lost and found box that probably have some random man's sweat dried into them? Nope, I'll pass, thanks."

"You can't say I didn't warn you about the dress being an issue with some of the jobs."

"It was quite obvious that you scribbled in *this* particular task right before you gave me the list."

"Cass is running a summer basketball clinic for a group of kids tomorrow. They need fresh nets, and besides, the view is great from down here."

Willa crossed one leg in front of the other and glowered at Brynn before she playfully threw the old net down towards her head. "My work will never get done with you watching my every move. Don't you have plans to take some aggression out on a punching bag?"

"Ha, yeah, I'll get right on that."

Willa received an unexpected sense of fulfillment from completing the menial tasks around different areas of the fitness center. It was something that she had never been exposed to with her career kicking off at such an early age. Even in her own condo, she hired people to do the more heavy-duty housework to allow extended time for her to be creative. She took great pleasure in checking off items on the list that was originally meant for Griffin, and even caught herself humming with satisfaction while cleaning the pool. The only thing left for her to do was to empty the trash in the bathrooms, which seemed the least appealing to her, so she saved it for last.

Willa pushed a cart around to each of the restrooms in the building, emptying the separate trash receptacles into the larger bins on the cart. After getting to all of the public bathrooms, she remembered, from spending so much time there when she was young, that there was a private bathroom for employees in the office behind the reception desk.

The overhead fluorescent lights crackled to life when she flipped the switch to the office area on. Two desks consumed the majority of space in the room. The one overflowing with protein powder samples and supplement bottles, with weightlifting motivational posters hung above it, she figured belonged to Griffin. The one lacking a chair and plastered with logo stickers from sponsored sporting goods companies had to belong to Brynn.

Willa recalled lots of dinner conversations when Mrs. Reed used to try to convince the twins to major in business so that they would someday run Mussels by the Sea. They both adamantly refused at the time, and yet ironically, they ended up there anyway.

The office space appeared to be smaller than when she last remembered. At first, she assumed that it was because everything seemed bigger when she was young, but after walking into the adjacent bathroom, she realized where the space went. One section of the office had been removed to expand the size of the bathroom. What used to be a tiny shower stall in the corner was now a huge walk in shower, large enough so that a fully tiled bench to sit on fit in the center of it. The entire space was altered to be wheelchair accessible.

Willa started to empty the trash in the room

as she did all the others, yet this one devastated her. The receptacle was filled with catheter bags. As she transferred them into the larger bin, she felt as though the pieces of herself that had just begun to heal were tearing apart all over again.

After learning about Brynn's diagnosis, Willa had spent hours upon hours in the university library researching spinal cord injuries. She had read about so many different aspects of the injury, including surgeries, therapies, and medications, but at the time, the inability to walk outweighed anything else in her mind. Over the years, she had all but forgotten the need to use a catheter to urinate. The remnants of them in the garbage brought the harsh reality back to Willa, especially that she had destroyed a woman's life before she ever got the opportunity to even live it.

A pounding started to build up in Willa's chest as her pulse increased and the constriction in her throat began to cut off the air from reaching her lungs. She rushed to the sink and splashed cold water on her face to help settle the panic attack that threatened to control her body. She blinked back at her reflection in the mirror until she felt calm again.

Having used the last remaining piece of paper towel to wipe the droplets of water from her face, she searched the cabinet below the sink for a replacement roll. In the process of using her fingertips to drag a roll forward from the back of the shelf, it hit a plastic container and knocked it out onto the floor. Willa picked up the bright red box marked with a red biohazard symbol on the front of it, along with the words 'Caution Sharps Disposal' printed below it. She gently shook the container and about a dozen empty syringes clanked around in the bottom of it. She replaced the container where she found it, supposing that there was a proper way to dispose of something like that which she wasn't aware of.

To top off an already distressing situation of finding the catheters, she now had to add on the thought of Brynn needing to inject herself with some sort of medication, regularly enough to require a sharps container with her at work.

After a night filled with unpleasant discoveries, Willa searched the gym for Brynn to let her know that the closing list was complete. The main areas of the fitness center were starting to quiet down now that it was getting to be later in the night, and only a few people remained in the cardio area. She made her way into the weightlifting room and found Brynn by herself.

A custom designed pull-up bar was made to be low enough for Brynn to reach it in her wheelchair. She sat below it with a fifty-pound weight leaning against her chest. Her chair was tipped backwards so that she was balanced on the two back wheels and she repeatedly pulled herself nearly to an upright position before tipping back again. Willa watched her from across the room, mesmerized by the pure strength that Brynn had in her upper body. She was perfectly sculpted and the power that she exuded with every movement seemed like an impossible feat to Willa, and yet Brynn kept the motion up repeatedly.

Willa continued to watch in awe as Brynn steadily pushed her body to the brink of exhaustion. Sweat poured down the sides of her face, which was locked in a determined scowl. The knuckles of her fingers, gripped tightly around the bar, were white and the veins in her wrists protruded out. Willa had no idea how many times Brynn was capable of repeating this motion, but something inside of herself told her that she had already surpassed her limit a long time ago.

She moved over to Brynn's side in hopes that her presence would end the repetitious torture that she was putting herself through. Brynn shot a determined look in Willa's direction, but then seemingly pushed herself to go faster. Willa boldly reached out and pulled one of the headphone earbuds out of Brynn's ear to get her attention, but still there was no response.

She knew that Brynn wasn't showing her a simple display of strength and neither was it a form of exercise or physical therapy. This was a release of pent up anger and sadness over the revelation they both had shared earlier. Willa couldn't wait until Brynn pushed her body to the brink of exhaustion, or worse, to the point of hurting herself. She took the risk of becoming the object of Brynn's anger, by stepping in front of her and placing a hand on the weight to make it nearly impossible for her to come back up.

"Give me a few more minutes and I'll be done," Brynn said through gritted teeth.

Willa shook her head, held Brynn firmly in place, and looked at her with a softness in her eyes. "It hurts to find out that he lied to you, and what the consequence of that has done to us, for *way* too many years."

Brynn clenched her jaw in protest. "I don't want to talk about this."

"You don't have to. I'm only asking that you find another way to deal with your emotions, because *this* scares me."

Brynn grasped each side of the large circular weight and lifted it with ease to her side, where she dropped it onto a stand. It settled into place with a thunderous bang as metal hit metal.

Willa felt a disconnect from Brynn as her blue eyes studied her with a piercing scrutiny. Brynn had done as she had asked, but now it was as if she was waiting for permission for her next move. Willa wasn't about to offer her another opening to self-destruct on herself, so instead she intertwined her fingers with Brynn's and gave her an understanding smile.

"How is it that you can be okay with what he's done?" Brynn asked.

"I'm not okay with it. There were so many times tonight that it invaded my thoughts. I could have allowed the anger to overwhelm me, but then I would be covering up all the marvelous feelings that you left me with tonight."

The corner of Brynn's mouth lifted and a luminous glow brightened up in her eyes. "Marvelous, huh?"

"Hmm." Willa leaned in and planted a kiss on Brynn's cheek, satisfied that the fury in her had subsided. "Don't let it go to your head," she added with a wink, before standing back upright and unwinding her fingers from Brynn's.

"I need a few minutes to clean up and then I can drive you back to the truck," Brynn said, already heading toward the doorway.

"Don't bother; you look like you need a nice long shower and I could use a little stroll."

"It's dark out already."

"Yes, but I'm parked right down the street and besides, with you in here, I know the sides of the road are safe from dangerous bikers," she said with a grin before walking away.

Chapter Twenty-two

"Ow, ow, ow!" Willa winced and buried her face into Megan's shoulder.

"All I'm cutting into is the stitches. I'm not even touching your skin, so calm down," Shannon assured her while bringing a tiny pair of surgical scissors close to Willa's knee.

"What about when you have to pull them out of my skin? You can't tell me that's going to feel very pleasant, now is it?" Willa whined.

"If you continue to squirm around, you're going to end up needing another set of stitches for the new wound that I'm about to cause."

"Now I see why you called me to be here." Megan rolled her eyes. "I can only imagine what it was like when you were putting them in."

"I had to call in my nurse practitioner on a weekend to come in and practically restrain her to the examination table."

"Hey," Willa pointed her finger, first at Shannon and then Megan, "both of you can stop discussing how big of a wuss I am any time now, especially since I'm right here."

"Okay, okay, let's change the subject," Megan agreed as she adjusted her hand. Willa realized that she was squeezing it so tight that the blood wasn't flowing into Megan's fingers under her frightened grip. "How about you tell us all about your date with Brynn?"

Willa's eyes widened and she turned abruptly to face Megan. "First of all, it wasn't *that* kind of a date and secondly, how did you know we were even together?"

"Maybe you didn't think it was a date, but Brynn most certainly must have. Don't forget, this is an awfully small town. Not only does word get around fast, but when you didn't show up at The Anchor for dinner alone, I knew the two you had to have gone somewhere together."

"Hmm, well, just because someone shows interest in another person, it doesn't mean that they're dating. I mean, my Aunt Beth thought that someone at the funeral had a crush on me, and I think she thinks it's you, Dr. Martin."

Shannon and Megan exchanged glances and then simultaneously broke out in laughter. Shannon finally took pity on Willa's pouty look of not being in on their exchange. "The day of the service, Brynn literally came to your rescue in your distraught state, and pushed aside anyone else in their effort to help you, so that she could be your heroine."

Willa scanned Megan's face with a questioning look to see if she agreed with Shannon's theory. "It's true; we all saw the same thing. That woman still has a thing for you after all these years," Megan agreed.

"I know she does." Willa let out a sigh.

"Do you not feel the same way?" Megan asked.

"It's not that I *don't*. It's more that so much has kept us apart and there are people who continue to do so, to the point that I wonder if it's worth even putting the effort into trying to be together."

"For a successful woman, you don't seem the type to let other people stand in the way of what you want."

"Not usually, but when one of those people happens to be her twin brother, whom she lives with and owns a business with, well, you get my point."

"In my opinion, if that man loved his sister half as much as he claims to, then he should let go of the past and let her be happy."

Shannon had been concentrating on Willa's knee, but she finally chimed in. "Please be careful around Griffin."

Megan arched over the edge of the table to get a better view of Shannon. "He definitely looks intimidating, but do you really think that he could be dangerous?"

Shannon didn't respond to Megan, but slowly and meticulously worked at removing another stitch.

"Good luck getting any further with her. The cryptic message is where it ends, but in case you were wondering, you never have to worry about your personal information being gossiped about by our friend here."

Shannon eyed Willa like a parent reprimanding a child by means of an expression, followed by a nod to show her loyalty not only to her friends, but also to her clientele.

"At least you know there won't be a tabloid story popping up about how you need a team of people to support you through a boo-boo," Megan teased.

"If I wasn't already crushing the life out of your fingers, I would find some other way to inflict pain on you."

"I deserve that. Just leave me the ability to pour a drink for us when we're done." Megan smirked at her own comment, but then her expression turned serious. "Speaking of drinks, I think I have a way to get some answers without drilling them illegally out of Shannon."

Soon after having survived the remaining stitch removal procedure, Willa followed Megan into The Anchor and took her usual seat at the bar. "So, tell me again, other than me getting a reward drink for not crying at the clinic, why are we here on your day off?"

Megan took the seat next to Willa and leaned in close to her ear. "This, my friend, is where you will see the power of what a great bartender is capable of." She waved her hand and within seconds, the guy behind the bar served them each a glass of Willa's favorite wine.

"While free alcohol on command is definitely a useful skill to have, I don't see how that's going to help us." Willa looked around at the empty bar, other than the old man, still in his usual corner seat.

"Be patient, and while we wait, tell me a little more about exactly what you need to know."

Willa settled into her barstool and took a long sip of her wine. She waited until the bartender was out of earshot and whispered, "There's a possibility that I wasn't to blame for Griffin not using his college scholarship."

"If you're not to blame, then that means he didn't stay to take care of his sister."

"Exactly, and if Shannon knows about it but can't say, then it has to be a medical reason."

"Can't you ask Brynn? I mean, she would know if her own twin brother was sick, wouldn't she?"

"I've been dealt a lot of verbal abuse from people all over town believing that I kept Laurel Cove's two star athletes from becoming something greater than local heroes that they were destined to be. Brynn truly believes that Griff stayed in order to help her through rehabilitation or else she wouldn't let that rumor spread around town."

"The answer you're searching for is something that I think I can get. Promise me that you'll let me do the talking, and if he gets confrontational, know that I won't let him physically harm you."

Willa's heart started racing with unknown anticipation. "Who are you talking about?"

"You'll see in a few seconds..." Megan turned her head to the door right before it opened, and Willa could tell by the sound of his boots that Craig had arrived for his daily dose of alcohol. Willa stiffened in her seat, but she felt a reassuring pat from Megan on her thigh, so she sat back and put her trust in Megan's supposed skills.

Craig grunted his dissatisfaction as he passed by Willa and took his place on the other side of Megan. The bartender on duty was preoccupied with making a drink for a customer dining out on the deck, so Craig impatiently pounded his knuckles on the counter to get his attention.

"I'll be with you in a second," the bartender barked back at him.

Craig turned to Megan. "You see the shit I gotta put up with when you ain't working?"

"Tony, hand me a bottle from the second shelf in the fridge," Megan ordered her bartender sternly.

Tony shot Craig a piercing glare, set down the martini that he was in process of building, grabbed a beer from the fridge, and shut the door with more force than required to close it. He handed the bottle to Megan and she reprimanded him with her icy gaze. With bartender precision, she popped the cap open using the side of the bar and a quick twisting motion of her wrist, before sliding it over to Craig. "I'm sorry for your trouble. Drinks are on the house today." Craig made an indiscernible grunt and gulped down a quarter of his bottle. For the time being, he was ignoring Willa and she let out a sigh of relief.

Willa generally believed herself to be a patient person. She used many opportunities during periods of having to wait to go over storylines in her head or to jot down notes for outlines. She rarely found a wasted moment in her day, when the lives of her characters swirled about in her mind constantly. The tension of waiting in suspense until Megan chose to make her move, though, was agonizingly slow, and didn't allow her to think of anything other than what might come of it. After watching Craig swallow down three beers and having Megan sit in complete silence next to her, Willa was ready to jump out of her own skin for a little relief from the anxiety of it all. She almost lost all hope, when Craig studied the clock on the wall and put his hands on the bar to push his stool back. As if right on cue, though, Tony brought out a plate with a juicy steak and a side of potatoes on it and set it down in front of Craig.

"Did I mention that a meal is on the house too?" Megan said casually without even looking in his direction.

Craig looked at the food suspiciously and almost continued to get up, but then with a little nod from Megan, Tony placed a cold bottle of beer on the bar. The drool was practically falling out of Craig's mouth, and that, paired with the bloody, rare steak, was a combination that had Willa holding in the need to gag. Craig stabbed the steak with his fork and crudely cut into it with the jagged knife, but Willa turned her face away so she didn't have to witness his display of open-mouthed chewing.

Finally, after what seemed like forever, Willa caught on to Megan's plan of action for a well-timed approach, when Craig had consumed enough steak to keep him there and wanting more, but not so much that he could be satisfied enough to leave. "You don't seem as torn up about the things being spread around the island about you as I thought you would," Megan casually let slip out.

The fork dropped from Craig's hand and landed in his plate with a clatter that sounded as though it had cracked the ceramic. The veins in his neck were already bulging as he turned it to drill Megan with an unnerving stare. "What're people saying 'bout me?" he demanded to know, as spittle sprayed from his dry, cracked lips.

Megan's fingertips shook when they reached for the stem of her glass, but she came off cool and collected when she spoke, as if without care, while seeming to be more interested in examining the display of liquor bottles behind the counter. "Now that Willa's made amends with Brynn, people are back to commending Griff for stepping up and taking care of his sister by sacrificing college."

Craig raised his beer bottle above his head. "Griff's a good guy, helping out an all," he said as he toasted the air and sucked down the rest of his beer.

"That he is, but the problem now is the focus is off Griff and people are wondering why you never used your scholarship. He's a hero for what he did, but what about you?"

"Why do they give a damn about me?"

"Because our top two local sports stars were

brought down by a tragedy. You were the next best chance Laurel Cove had at fame and they want to know why you failed us. The idea has even been thrown around that you were too scared to play at a collegiate level without Griff there to back you up."

Craig's face was already a reddish tint from too much sun exposure out on the boat, but it slowly increased into a bright crimson color the more enraged he got. "If that's how they're judging us, then they need to know that Griff ain't no saint."

Megan revealed just enough of her face to Willa for her to see the wink that she flashed to her, before she faced Craig for the first time during their conversation. "It would be a shame for *your* name to be the one people mention as the town disappointment," she taunted him.

The barstool made a screeching sound as Craig scratched its legs across the hardwood floor on his way off it. His breath, thick with alcohol, weighed heavy in the air as he stood over Megan and made his demand. "Make sure that every person on this piece of shit island knows that Griffin Reed failed his physical exam because of steroid use. The University didn't accept his scholarship." Craig stormed out of The Anchor and slammed the door behind him.

"And that is how the combination of the right amount of alcohol, a full belly, and a few perfectly timed social cues can lead to finding out just about anything you need to know."

Willa leaned in and gave her friend a hug so tight that she could hear Megan gasp for breath. "If the CIA knew you had skills like that, they'd steal you away from this small town."

"Ah, but I could never leave the luxurious smell

of fish bait that my customers so generously provide me with daily."

"Strangely enough, you do miss it when it's not in your life," Willa said solemnly, in remembrance of her father, then she hopped down from her barstool in a hurry, and pulled her keys from her purse.

"Where are you off to in such a rush?"

"News travels fast on this island. I'd rather have Brynn hear the latest revelation about her brother from me."

Chapter Twenty-three

At least one person doing some sort of activity occupied every room at Mussels by the Sea. Willa checked each room twice, thinking that she might have just crossed paths with Brynn in her search for her, but she still didn't come across her anywhere. The only person who looked like she might have a clue as to her whereabouts was a young woman in a bright red bathing suit, sitting on top of a lifeguard chair overseeing the indoor pool area.

"It's only my responsibility to keep track of the kids in the water, not to babysit my boss," she said, snapping a wad bubble of gum, which echoed throughout the tiled room. Willa rolled her eyes and shook her head as she walked away, feeling as though her clothes would hold the distinct odor of chlorine for the rest of the day.

As she headed through the main room of the fitness center, the wall of lockers caught Willa's eye and she took a chance at opening her father's locker. Inside was the lobster mug, washed clean from the last time she used it, so she grabbed it and fled towards the trail behind the building.

Stopped at the end of the wooden ramp to wipe the perspiration from her brow and to catch her breath, Willa decided that she would have to dedicate some time to returning to her cardio routine, when her life returned to its regular schedule. The idea of what her life was like a few days ago compared to now seemed so drastically different and it was almost difficult to remember the structured schedule that she set for herself to keep on task for projects. With the arrival of new friendships, a chaos of other responsibilities was brought with them, and she quite enjoyed the randomness of her days. One of those friendships, the most unexpected, was a rekindled one that Willa was eternally grateful for. She watched her now, by the water's edge, a fishing pole in one hand and a book in the other. The sun left streaks of shimmering light against Brynn's short black hair. Willa wrestled with the idea of wanting to take out her cellphone and snap a photo of her, so that she could capture the moment to keep forever, but instead she opted to savor it as it was happening.

"Are you planning on coming down here to join me, or are you just going to stare at me from a distance?" Brynn asked without taking her focus off the book.

"How did you know I was here?"

"All the fish in the sea were scared away by the sound of you clicking down the ramp in those high heels of yours."

Willa made her way over to the picnic table, where she set down the mug, poured herself a cup of coffee, and refilled Brynn's cup. She held the steaming mug out for her. "I didn't mean to stare, but I don't ever think I'll get used to seeing you reading a book."

"You'd better get used to it, because as long as you continue to write books, I'll keep reading them."

"All of them, even the ones I write for young adults?"

"Especially the series you did about the teenagers

that turn into owls at night."

"You and Dad seriously read all of those?"

"Yup. I'm still hoping there'll be a spinoff that might continue to show how they end up as adults."

"Ugh, it was horrible enough dragging out the storyline to nine novels about those same damn kids, but the fans loved that crap, so my publisher kept pushing for more."

"Oh, come on, when that one girl, Solena, flew away at the end, you literally left the story up in the air."

"What would you want to have happen to her?"

"I'd like to think that eventually she would find her way home again, back to where the people who love her are waiting."

"I'm sure that's where she'll end up." Willa kicked off her heels, let them drop to the ground, and propped her bare feet up on the wheel of Brynn's chair.

"You had the stitches removed," Brynn observed as she ran her fingertip over the freshly healed cut.

"Mm-hmm, hopefully the scar gets less noticeable over time."

"It should as long as you're careful not to rip it open again." Brynn closely inspected the wound site. "See how it's already tearing at the end here."

Willa's eyes widened with fear and she clutched at her knee, as she tried to see the cut.

A fit of chuckles escaped from Brynn and she dropped the fishing pole in the midst of her uncontrollable laughter. When Willa figured out that she was the victim of another infamous Brynn prank, she crossed her arms below her chest and glared at her relentlessly until the smile faded from her face.

"Keep this up and Meg will be happy to know

that you're offering to take her place as my official hand holding support partner during all of my future doctor appointments."

"I really need my hands to get around with, so how about we compromise and I let you squeeze my leg for support?" Brynn suggested, keeping a stoically serious expression.

Willa attempted to hold out as long as she could, not wanting to give in to Brynn's question, which in itself had another joke hidden within it. It became nearly impossible, though, for her to keep up with a hard as nails glare, when Brynn's eyes narrowed to crinkled slits because her grin took over too much of her face. She had no choice but to break their visual contest out of fear of turning to mush under Brynn's captivating stare. She distracted herself by hopping down from the table to pick up the fallen fishing pole. "Next time I'd rather hold your hand than Meg's. Besides, no matter how much pain I'm in, I doubt that I could ever break those strong hands of yours," she added shyly, pretending that reeling in the line was distracting her.

Brynn's humor was set aside as she said seriously, "Any time you need me, I'll be there for you." She let a few moments pass by, and the truth of her statement sunk in with Willa before she added, "Even for helping you with things like letting you know that you're spinning the spool in the wrong direction."

"Yeah, well, you've been on that same page since I first got here."

"Let's trade then," Brynn proposed, holding the book out and reaching for the pole.

Willa accepted the offer and settled back in her spot on the table to read from her own story to

Brynn, while she cast the line with the finesse of an expert. The words flowed from Willa's mouth with only the background sound of the lure dragging below the surface of the water and the whoosh of the line as Brynn released it back out again. They continued like this in a peaceful duo of narrator and angler, until Willa reached the end of the chapter and Brynn announced that she should be heading back to the fitness center.

Willa closed the book and nervously bit at her lower lip as she ran her fingers over the edges of the pages. The apprehension that Willa had at the concept of them having to part ways was evident in her slow methodical movements.

"Cass has a private tennis lesson that I need to prep the court for. We can meet up later, though. How about if you come to my place and I can throw some ribs on the barbecue?"

"That sounds lovely." Willa hesitated, not knowing how to bring up the accusation. "But, there's a reason why I came looking for you down here."

"What is it, Willa?" Brynn's serious tone mirrored her own.

"Craig confirmed to me and Meg that Griff didn't pass his physical exam into college because he tested positive for steroids."

The serenity of the atmosphere remained, but any sense of it disappeared from Brynn's expression as the truth clouded her mind with so many years of misconceptions. Without uttering a single word, Brynn went about cleaning up the area. First, she meticulously attached the hook onto one of the guide holes along the pole and neatly placed it into the shed and locked it in. Then she poured out the remainder of the coffee from the thermos and two mugs and placed them in her bag.

When it came time to take the book back, Willa could see that Brynn was doing all she could to not explode with anger.

She lowered herself down to the bench seat and placed the book in Brynn's lap, but didn't release her hands from it yet so that she couldn't just take it and leave. "I can't even begin to imagine how hurt you must be."

Brynn's eyes raked over the flat stones below her chair with disdain. She clenched her jaw so tight that it hardly moved when she spoke. "Every single penny that I earned, I gave to Griff. He made me believe that I had stolen his future away from him."

"He was probably so embarrassed by what happened that you became the perfect excuse for him, without having to reveal that he was rejected."

"Why are you defending him? This affected you as much as it did me."

"I'm not defending him. I just want to wait until he gets back to put my energy towards being enraged. We can face him together, if you'd want to?"

Brynn shook her head and finally looked directly at Willa. "I don't trust him around you. He'll blame you for his secret being exposed and that's not safe."

Even through the thick book between them, Willa could feel Brynn's body tense up and visibly see it as she shifted uncomfortably in her chair, ready to erupt from the seat with agitation. "I'd say Griff is the one who needs to be afraid of *you*."

"Damn right, he better be."

"He had better hope there's a flight of stairs between you and him when you have this conversation."

The tension eased in Brynn's body as her shoulders dropped back down to a relaxed state and her mouth turned up just enough for her smirk to emerge. "Of course you would choose now to implement our joke deal."

"I'm willing to do just about anything to get you to calm down."

"*Anything*?" Brynn repeated slowly, her eyes glimmering with a mischievous need.

Willa took each of Brynn's hands in her own and slid to the very edge of the bench so that their knees were touching. She leaned in and stared intensely into Brynn's piercing blue eyes. "If I kiss you, can you promise me that you won't take your anger out on your own body?"

The slightest movement from Brynn's head was enough of an agreement for Willa and she took no time at all to lean in and press her lips against Brynn's.

What had begun, in Willa's mind, as a quick kiss to take Brynn's mind off all the negative thoughts surrounding her brother turned into a sensation of pure bliss. Brynn's full lips consumed her own with a tenderness that she couldn't pull away from. She found herself coming up off her seat to get closer.

Willa's lips were pried open gently by the tip of Brynn's tongue. She allowed Brynn to linger within the cavern of her mouth just long enough for the silky rubbing of their tongues against one another to tease her. When Willa started to feel dizzy with desire, she slowly pulled away, leaving one last peck on Brynn's still protruding lips.

She tucked a stray strand of her blonde hair back behind her ear and released a snicker when she noticed that her pink lipstick had smeared onto Brynn's lips. She used her thumb to wipe away the evidence of their kiss.

"Ahem." Willa bashfully cleared her throat and stood up, needing to separate from Brynn before she might uncontrollably go back for more. "Work is waiting for you, and I should be going, so I'll see you tonight then?"

A blissful smile swept over Brynn's face and Willa was satisfied that any thoughts about Griffin would be wiped away by the power of the moment shared between them.

Chapter Twenty-four

A strong gust of wind blew, making the dock sway with even more force than the waves below it did, as Willa steadily made her way to the end of it. She was glad that she traded in her heels for a pair of sneakers and her dress for yoga pants during her little excursion to the docks. Rows of lobster boats were already lined up and some of the owners were wiping them down after a long morning and afternoon out on the sea. She received a few courteous waves from the men who worked alongside her father for many years.

The perfectly maintained white and red boat with the name *The Elaine* stenciled across the back of it stood out among all the others. The reminder of her mother's name, forever a part of her history, was bittersweet now that her father was added to that list.

She sat on the rail of the boat and swung her legs over onto the deck. For a heavily used workboat, even the platform was meticulously clean. She made her way to the cabin and stood behind the wheel, picturing her father's hands on it as he navigated across the ocean around the Cove. Willa pulled the boat key out of her sweatshirt pocket and played with the buoy keychain attached to it. She toyed with the idea of starting up the boat and taking it around the harbor, but she hadn't driven a boat in twenty years and she never went alone, even then.

The boat was useless to Willa and she knew that

it would be a shame to let it rot away sitting at the dock.

She went around the cabin, picking through any personal items that remained there and filled her purse with them. There were a lot of little trinkets hanging up that her father had called his good luck charms. She smiled as she gathered up the faux fur rabbit's foot, the little metal horseshoe, and the plastic hula danger girl that had hips that bobbled with every movement of the boat. The last item that she noticed in the cabin was an old photograph taped to the window. Willa figured that he must have placed it there after she had left, because the last time she had seen it, the picture was inside one of their photo albums. The image brought tears to her eyes as she stared at a picture of herself, Griffin, and Brynn posing in front of a stack of lobster traps. Griffin was in his traditional stance, showing off his muscles, and Brynn was pretending that her arm was stuck in one of the traps. Willa had always seen herself in photos as the boring one, standing straight and smiling at the camera, but in this particular one, she was staring directly at Brynn's and her foolish antics. A huge smile covered her face, frozen in a moment of time, caught in pure joy at the prank of her beloved friend. The emotions welled up inside of her, as she thought about how her father loved the three of them so much that he wanted to keep their image close by as he worked each day.

With a heavy heart, Willa placed a for sale sign at the front of the boat. On her way off it, though, she lost the nerve to leave just yet, and sank down onto the wooden deck. She pulled the hood of her sweatshirt tight around her face and lay, facing the sky, and let the motion of the waves lull her into a meditative state. When the time came for her to rise up and climb out, she felt at peace enough with her decision to let the boat go without regret.

At the end of the dock, Willa decided to make the short walk to The Anchor instead of back to her car. She hoped that Megan might still be at the bar and she could celebrate the first big step that she had taken towards finalizing her father's estate. A wave of disappointment swept through her, though, when it was only Tony behind the bar and the same old man in the corner. She started to turn back, when a voice came from across the room.

"You smell like the sea today."

Willa squinted as she tried to adjust to the dim lighting in the bar to confirm that the usually quiet old man had called out to her. Sure enough, when she looked to the corner, he was staring right at her over his beer mug. "This restaurant is literally built on top of the ocean; everything smells like the sea," she pointed out to him.

"Ah, every other time you've come in here, you smell like flowers that spray out of a bottle. This time you smell like a true islander that has been out on the sea."

Willa raised her arm up high enough to sniff the sleeve of her sweatshirt, hoping that it was the salt in the air that he was referring to and not the scent of fish.

When the old man noticed what she was doing, he waved his hand in the air to stop her. "Quit that foolishness; you smell fine. Your daddy always used to say he was raising the spitting image of his wife. Henry was right. There's no part of him in you at all."

Willa shot him a disgusted glare, planted her hands on her hips, and let out an insulted huff.

He let out a laugh that sounded more like a

department store Santa Claus than a drunk man in a bar. "That ain't no insult if you knew how lovely your mama was."

"You knew my mother?" Willa asked, letting her guard down a little.

"Oh yeah, Henry, Elaine, and I have history together that goes way back. We were as close as you and the Reed twins used to be."

Willa yearned to know more about her mother, but her father didn't like to talk about anything in the least bit sentimental, so she stopped asking questions about her when she was young. This stranger was the first person that seemed willing to offer a window to her past. She rounded the corner of the bar and took the seat next to him. "How is it that you claim to be such great friends with my family and yet I don't ever recall meeting you before?"

"After Elaine passed, neither one of us could bear to spend time around each other. That woman was the glue that held us together. Without her, nothing was the same." He held out his hand to Willa. "Name's Blake by the way."

Willa shook his offered hand that was dry and hard to the touch, most likely from years of working on a boat. "Did you have a falling out of sorts?"

"Nothing like that. We had each other's back if the other needed it, but we kept our distance."

"Can I ask you what she was like?"

"She was the most intelligent person I'd ever met. Her family spent summers here; owned one of them big houses on the cove. She'd sneak out and come meet Henry and me down by the docks when we were teenagers. Her parents despised us island boys. Said we were good for nothing and a bad influence on their little angel."

Blake went to wet his mouth with a sip of beer, but he was already at the bottom of the mug. Willa motioned for Tony to refill it for him.

Blake continued, "We went a few years without seeing her while she was overseas at college in England, but one day she showed up as if she'd never left. This time, her parents couldn't control her every move. When she married Henry, though, they disowned her, but she was happier than she'd ever been. That girl wasn't born here, but she was an islander all the same. She loved the sea almost as much as Henry and I did."

Willa motioned towards Blake's beer. "At least you had the sense to retire, unlike Dad."

"No true lobsterman gives up on the sea, not by choice, anyway. The motor blew on my boat and the insurance won't cover it."

"You'd still be working if you could?"

"It's the only way I can afford to keep my house. Retirement check won't cover that. I'm just biding my time until they take it from me."

Willa reached into her purse and clasped her fingers around the little buoy key chain. When she opened up her hand, she was holding it out to Blake. "Please take *The Elaine* so that you can do what you love."

Blake looked at the key with a flushed face and shook his head. "I can't." He shook his head in protest. "That boat was his pride and joy."

"And it will rot away if someone doesn't use it, or it will be sold to someone who won't respect her the way I know you would."

"Oh, Miss Barton, I would take good care of her."

Willa set the keys in his hand. "All I ask of you in

return is two things."

"Anything you need, I'll do it."

"The first is that you'll keep the boat named *The Elaine*."

"Of course. I cared for her almost as much as Henry did. The boat will forever be a memorial to her."

Willa nodded her thanks. "The other thing is that you will promise to sell lobsters to the Bennetts at the Sea Turtle Inn at a reduced rate so that they can stay in business."

"Not a problem. John and Martha are good people. It'd be my pleasure to help them out."

Willa got down from her stool, grateful that she wouldn't have to sell the boat to a stranger. "Do you think that maybe someday you could tell me some more stories about my parents?"

Blake pointed to his head. "Oh, I have some great ones saved up in here for you."

"I'm looking forward to it."

As Willa put her hand on the door to leave, Blake called out to her.

"Hey, what I said earlier, about you being just like your mother, I was wrong. You've got Henry's heart in you too."

Chapter Twenty-five

Willa raised her hand to knock on Brynn's door, but there was a note taped to it, instructing her to go to the back patio. It was there that she found Brynn busily applying a coat of marinade to a rack of ribs. "Mmm, it smells delicious," Willa complemented as a breeze wafted some of the smoke in her direction.

"Yeah, I've kind of perfected the art of cooking out on the barbecue. Griff and I have a deal that half the year I do the cooking out here and the other half he does it in the kitchen."

"Griff in the kitchen making something other than protein shakes? I can't imagine that."

"He doesn't have much of an option if we want something cooked on the stove. It's too high up for me to see what I'm doing and there's too much of a risk of me getting burned."

"Was the transition difficult, having to relearn the world from a whole different perspective?"

"Essentially, I got shorter, wider, and only able to roll, which was enough of a challenge, but I also had to adjust to the concept of leaving behind high school and becoming an adult all at the same time. The psychological aspect of my injury was more damaging than the physical side of it."

"It didn't help that your best friend ditched you either, did it?" Willa nervously bit at her bottom lip.

Brynn rubbed her hand at the base of Willa's back. "Hey, we both know who's to blame for that and it's neither one of us. I have you here now, and that's all that matters to me."

Willa noticed place settings set up on the patio table next to the grill. "There's a game on tonight. Why don't we eat in the living room like we always used to?"

"You hate watching sports on the television. Even at my live games, your face was buried in a book."

"Between Griff's games and yours, it was the only time that I had to get homework done for the three of us. I doubt any of us would have graduated if I hadn't done that. Besides, I miss watching you get excited over watching a game."

"You like to watch me yell at the screen?"

"Mm-hmm, it's very entertaining."

"Ha, well, I'll finish up here while you move our little party inside."

⧓ ⧓ ⧓ ⧓

Willa sank back into the couch with a full stomach and wiped the remnants of the barbecue sauce off her fingers with a napkin. She smiled as she watched Brynn point a rib bone at the television as one of the players hit a ball high in the air towards the back of the stadium. When it dropped down into the stands and the crowd began to roar, Brynn pumped her fist into the air and let out a congratulatory shout. Willa sighed in contentment.

Brynn finished her last bite of food, and Willa scooped up her plate. Brynn reached to release the brake on her wheelchair, but Willa stopped her.

"It's the last inning. You finish watching while I

clean up."

Willa placed the last dry dish in the cupboard. She found that everything was in the same general place that it had been located back when she was young, helping Ms. Reed put away the dishes after dinner, except now everything was kept in the lower shelves and drawers so that they were accessible to Brynn.

By the time the game ended, and Brynn entered the kitchen, Willa was blowing across the surface of her mug of hot tea while leaning against the counter. She smiled after her first sip and pointed out the second mug that was waiting for Brynn on the table.

"You've been quieter than usual tonight," Brynn observed.

"I gave away Dad's boat today."

"That's not an easy task to deal with."

Willa shook her head to show that it wasn't.

Brynn approached her, took the steaming mug out of her hands, and set it on the counter. Before Willa could comprehend what was happening to her, Brynn had swept one arm under her legs and the other around her waist to pull Willa into her lap. Willa gasped with delight at how weightless Brynn had made her feel with her strong arms supporting her, but within seconds, a kiss suppressed the sounds escaping from her mouth. Willa wrapped an arm around Brynn's neck to pull her closer and deepen the kiss.

She held Brynn's chin back to separate from her long enough to ask, "What's all this about?"

"When I was feeling down, twice before, you cheered me up with a kiss. I hoped it would have the same effect on you."

"Mmm, more please."

They joined once again, lips pressed together,

tongues dancing from one mouth to the other, and nipping playfully at each other's skin. Willa was so overwhelmed with the energy between them, that she didn't realize that Brynn had stopped kissing until she opened her eyes to see the intense blue of Brynn's irises inches from her own.

"May I kiss you everywhere?" Brynn asked, her face riddled with sincerity.

Willa nodded her approval before dipping her head into Brynn's neck, not wanting to break their physical connection. She was in the process of leaving a row of delicate kisses along Brynn's neckline, when she became aware that they were in motion. Brynn's hand safely tucked her legs to the side as they squeezed through the doorway into what used to be Ms. Reed's room but now must belong to her daughter.

In one swift movement, Brynn lifted Willa onto the bed and seconds later, Brynn pressed her body against Willa's. Brynn commanded a powerful presence with her upper body hovering above her. Willa ran her hands down the length of Brynn's arms, taking in every accented curve of each muscle. She had been admiring her arms for days and to have full access to them made her dizzy with desire. Brynn winked at her from above and Willa blushed at the idea that she was aware of how turned on she was just by the perfectly sculpted muscles of her arms.

Brynn showed off how powerful they were, by bracing all of her weight on one arm to simultaneously lower herself to kiss Willa while using the other to unzip her sweatshirt. At the memory of earlier in the day, Willa became self-conscious of the comment that Blake said to her. "Blake told me that I smelled like the sea because I was out on the boat."

Disapproval gleamed in Brynn's eyes. "And since when do you take the word of a drunken old man for advice on the scent of a woman?" She twisted one lock of Willa's curly hair around her finger, lifted it to her nose, and inhaled with the intensity of someone properly testing the aroma of a fine wine. "You have nothing to worry about."

Brynn sat up and pulled Willa upright with her. She kept her occupied with kisses long enough to remove her sweatshirt, blouse, and bra before using her palm against Willa's chest to guide her back down to the pillow. Willa seemed surprised at how quickly Brynn exposed her from the waist up, when she glanced down at Brynn circling her bare nipple under her thumb. She grasped at the comforter to get some sort of cover for herself, but it was too taut to pull it around her body. Brynn pulled her fingers from the comforter and Brynn kissed each one. "You're absolutely gorgeous," Brynn whispered before sucking her nipple into her mouth.

Willa moaned and arched her back, pushing her breast further into Brynn's mouth. After a few minutes of watching Brynn's pleasure at moving from one breast to the other until the flickering motion of her tongue brought them alive, she felt a hand wander down to the waistband of her yoga pants. In one fluid motion, Brynn had managed to slide both her pants and her underwear down to her ankles. Willa gave her a scolding look, but went along with it and helped by kicking them the rest of the way off as well as her socks.

They actually knew each other's bodies quite well from years of gym locker rooms and changing in front of one another during a countless number of sleepovers, but the intimate touches that Brynn was now bestowing on every inch of her inner thigh made

Willa feel as though Brynn's feelings had run deeper for longer than she had believed. Willa reached her fingertips down and brushed them on Brynn's cheek to still her for a moment. "When did you first know?"

A flash of recognition swept across her face and the words, "Since the beginning," flowed out of Brynn's mouth.

Willa could tell that the release of such an emotional statement was out of the ordinary for Brynn and she was now struggling with the aftermath of how to deal with it. Willa didn't want to scare Brynn off from any future moments of sharing her true emotions with her, so she decided to help distract her from what she had revealed. Willa slid her legs up and spread them open as wide as they would go and guided Brynn's head down between them. She was sure that she could feel a smile spread across Brynn's lips just before they wrapped around her clit.

Two hands came up underneath Willa and held her firmly in place while she writhed in ecstasy as Brynn's tongue played out a steady rhythm that she could feel vibrate throughout her entire body. She was only partially perceptive of the sounds of pleasure that were escaping out of her own mouth, which caused Brynn to increase in pressure and speed.

When she thought that Brynn couldn't possibly be any more attentive to her needs, she began to feel one of her fingers enter inside of her, ever so slowly, as if Brynn was exploring her one millimeter at a time. Willa wanted more and faster, so she attempted to slide down onto her finger to push it in deeper. Brynn wasn't about to give in so easily, though, as she moved back with her.

"I know what you *think* you want, but trust me,

this will be better," Brynn insisted between swirls of her tongue.

It didn't take long for the sensation of the circular motion that Brynn was making just barely inside of her to overcome Willa. "Oh," was all she could manage to say, as her body shook with the fury of the orgasm as she let herself go.

Brynn stayed between her legs long enough to settle the tiny convulsions that continued after her release, but Willa soon found herself swept up into her arms in a comforting embrace. Her friend that had always provided the brute strength and protection when she needed it now showed a gentle side that held her as though she were made of porcelain. She settled in the warmth of her arms until her breathing returned to normal.

When their lips collided together once more, Willa could taste herself mixed in with Brynn's kisses and it made her crave for her turn to give the same attention back to Brynn. Willa lifted the bottom of Brynn's shirt and placed her palm against the perfectly chiseled abs hidden underneath. A burning heat radiated from her skin and it excited Willa to free her from the shirt that held it in. Before she could, though, a firm hand stopped her from lifting it up. Willa looked into Brynn's eyes and smiled warmly before trying again, but once more, Brynn denied her access to remove the barrier that separated them.

"Please," she pleaded as the desire built up inside of her.

Brynn shook her head and covered Willa's hand to block her from trying again. "Not this time," she said quickly and attempted to cover up her words with kisses to Willa's brow to avoid an explanation.

"Why?" Willa asked, dodging the distraction.

"Can I taste you again?"

"I'd like to make you feel as good as I do. Please let me." She waited for a moment but Brynn turned her face from her. Willa guided her chin back in her direction with her free hand. "If there's something in particular that you need me to know or do for you, just tell me and we can do this together."

"I don't want to, okay?" Brynn snapped at her coldly.

Willa sat up higher against the headboard, covered her breasts with one arm, and closed her legs together tightly. She became self-conscious at being the only one nude, and without the comfort of Brynn surrounding her, she needed to get away. In a hurried frenzy, she leapt from the bed, gathered up her clothes in her arms, and rushed from the room.

In the bathroom down the hall, she searched for a washcloth under the sink and once again came across another sharps container rattling with needles and she silently cursed the damage that she had caused to Brynn, even more so now that it somehow affected her physical relationship with her.

After cleaning herself up and getting clothed again, she opened the door and made her way to the kitchen, where her shoes and purse were waiting for her, but also Brynn. She silently slipped on her sneakers and slung her purse sloppily over her shoulder in a mess of straps tangled together with stray strands of her hair.

"Don't go," Brynn said, devoid of emotion, which she was clearly hiding deep within herself.

"Are you ready to be open with me about what happened in there?"

Brynn stared fixedly at the counter beyond where Willa was standing and didn't respond.

"That's what I thought." Willa put her hand on the door to the backyard. Her car was in the front, but she didn't want to risk Brynn convincing her to stay. Brynn not trusting her enough to be honest with her already hurt her too much, and she wanted to get away as soon as possible. "Goodnight, Brynn," she said before closing the door behind her.

Chapter Twenty-six

"Ow, do you have to poke at it that hard?" Willa whined.

Shannon prodded the skin as she examined the scar on Willa's knee with scrutiny. "I have to be sure if you think that it might be infected, although I don't see any signs of it. What were the symptoms that you told the nurse again?"

"Um, pain and swelling…"

"Does it hurt even when I'm not touching it?"

"Uh huh, sometimes…"

"It doesn't look swollen now. It actually looks like it's healing quite nicely."

"Oh, well, it comes and goes."

Shannon's eyes narrowed as she stood and watched Willa squirm around on the exam table, causing the paper sheet to crinkle under her movements.

"If you're concerned, then it might be best if we start you on antibiotics just to be sure." Shannon pulled out a pad of prescription paper and began scribbling something on it.

"Antibiotics?"

"Yes. It will stop any infection that you might have, although you have to be careful of the side effects."

"Side effects?"

"You don't have to worry about most of them, but it is quite common for women to get yeast infections while taking them," Shannon mentioned, handing the prescription to Willa.

Willa waved her hand at the piece of paper in rejection. "On second thought, if it looks okay to you, maybe I should pass on the antibiotics."

Shannon eyed Willa, her expression sharp with intelligence. "Very well then," she said as she folded the prescription in half and tucked it away in her lab coat pocket. "So, now that's taken care of, is there anything *else* you needed to see me about?"

"Now that you mentioned it, since you happen to be a doctor, I did have a medical question I wanted to ask you about."

"I thought there might be something on your mind," Shannon said, rolling her seat closer to the exam table and tapping the lever so that it raised up to Willa's level.

Willa played with the hem of her dress until she worked up the nerve to ask, "Are there things that might prevent a person who is a paraplegic from being able to have intercourse?"

A serious expression swept over Shannon's face and she tapped Willa's good knee with the bottom of her clipboard. "You know I can't answer that."

"I'm just asking in general, not about anyone in particular."

"Every case is different, so much, in fact, that if I were to give you any insight at all, it would be obvious that it was tailored to the situation that you're in. We both know whom it's referring to and that is a serious breach of my confidentiality code. I could lose my medical license for sharing that information."

"It was wrong of me to ask that of you, I'm sorry. I shouldn't have come to see you. My leg is fine."

Willa started to get down from the table, but Shannon placed her hand on her arm to hold her back. "Wait a minute. Just because I can't divulge certain information doesn't mean that I can't help you with some advice. Tell me what happened."

Willa struggled to come up with a way to explain what she perceived had taken place the previous night without sharing the personal details of their time together. "Brynn wants to be with me, but she won't let me reciprocate back in the same way. It terrifies me to think that something I don't even remember doing twenty years ago may have caused her the inability to be intimate with someone..." her voice began to crack, "especially me."

"Without seeming too vague, I can promise that what you are specifically worried about is *not* an issue. Now, I'm not saying that there aren't going to be things that you will need to do differently than in an able-bodied relationship, but the biggest hurdle for the two of you is the communication that has to happen beforehand."

"She didn't open up to me when I asked, even afterwards." Willa wiped away a trickle of tears that had run down her cheek. "And the worst part is that I walked out on her because of it. She might not ever want to talk to me again at this point."

Shannon handed her a tissue. "Go find Brynn and see if she'd be willing to come back here with you. I could facilitate a medical conversation with the both of you so that you might get a better understanding of what her needs are for a sexual relationship to occur between you."

Willa's face scrunched up in anguish. "I think I'd have better luck getting her to go to a ballet dance with me."

Shannon snickered as she tried to hold back a laugh.

"At least you think my situation is amusing," Willa stated smugly.

"Oh, Willa, I'm laughing because what you don't see is that the two of you know each other so well that it has put a barrier up between you. You are taking what was once an innocent childhood friendship and jumping to an adult physical relationship; there are bound to be insecure moments for both of you, but you'll get through it. Just talk to her."

Soon after leaving the clinic, with Shannon's advice still fresh in her mind, Willa searched the fitness center, determined to at least make plans with Brynn to talk. Once again, she found herself roaming from room to room on a hunt for Brynn, only to come across random people in the midst of their workout routines. When she entered the basketball court, she got her hopes up at the sound of someone located at the far end of the room.

Willa had almost reached the end of the bleachers, when Cassidy stood up after retrieving a stray ball from under the stands. She came to an abrupt stop, her heels squealing on the smooth surface, but it was too late to turn back, because Cassidy had already caught sight of Willa and was rapidly approaching her.

"Brynn is a fucking mess today and I know you're to blame, so it would be in your best interest to walk out now before you make things worse."

For a split second, Willa almost did what Cassidy asked, but something held her frozen to the spot. "There was a time when you and Brynn were a couple, right?" Willa averted her eyes to the floor, not daring to make eye contact with Cassidy.

"Yes, until you got in the way of things."

Willa momentarily forgot her fear as it turned to confusion. "According to Brynn, that was years ago. How could I have possibly gotten in the way?"

"We went to the movies to see that ridiculous children's story you wrote about teenagers that turn into owls at nighttime."

Willa held in a smirk as she watched Cassidy get exasperated while trying to describe her film. "The first one?" She asked for clarification.

Cassidy's face turned red with frustration. "Yeah, I guess. Why does it matter?"

"Because there were nine movies in the series. It might be essential to the story you're telling me to know which one you're referring to."

Cassidy's irritation level rose to a new level as evident by the way she was seemingly crushing the basketball between her hands, so Willa decided to back down and let her finish without interruption.

"During the movie at the part when that girl got her wings for the first time, I looked over and there were tears in Brynn's eyes."

Willa waited long enough to make sure that Cassidy was done talking, and so that she could decipher what she meant by it. "It was a kind of emotional part of the movie, don't you think?"

"Maybe for a ten-year-old, but we're talking about Brynn, who cries as often as a brick might."

"Okay, I agree with you on that, but how did that ruin your relationship with her?"

"Because it became painfully clear to me then that if the only thing that could move her to tears was something you wrote, then there was no chance that I could ever compete with you."

"If you've come to terms with that and moved on, why do you keep chasing me away from her?"

"Because I'm the one left behind to deal with her pain when you decide to go back to your Hollywood lifestyle and leave her again." Cassidy turned and started towards the rack to put the basketball away.

"Wait, please..." Willa called after her. "I promise I'll never leave her, not like I did before, anyway."

Cassidy's head drooped and she turned back to Willa, turning the ball over in her hands and testing it for air pressure. "It would destroy her if you did."

"None of my other relationships ever worked out, and I believe it's because in my heart I was always waiting to come back to her. I guess I never believed that she would accept me into her life again," Willa openly confessed what she had held in for so long. She assumed it came so easily because Cassidy was quite possibly the only other person who had ever cared for Brynn the way that she did.

"I'm glad you made amends for her sake, but something must have happened between you two. She's so upset that I sent her to the office because I was afraid that she might puncture the heavy bag with her fist."

"I'm trying to fix what happened." Willa sighed, thinking that asking Cassidy for help was simultaneously the worst idea and her only hope. "Can you please tell me why she won't let me get close to her physically?"

Cassidy's body stiffened and she violently shook her head. "It's not my place to tell you what to do in bed."

"Please, Cass, you're the only one I know that has

been with her in that way and I think she's embarrassed to talk to me about it." Willa's shoulders dropped and she added softly, "I just want to make her happy without having to force her into a conversation that I know she's too proud to have."

"Fine, I'll let you in on what the problem is, for Brynn's sake." Cassidy stepped in closer to Willa and lowered her voice. "Spur of the moment lovemaking doesn't work well for her because she needs time prior to sex to empty her bladder. If she doesn't, it could mean the possibility of an accident, which you can imagine is quite embarrassing for her."

Willa's face lit up for the first time all day. "That's it, I mean, everything else works the way it should?"

Cassidy raised her eyebrows at the overly excited woman in front of her. "Yeah, you didn't break that part of her, at least."

Willa glared at her, but she was too elated to dwell on the jab that she had thrown at her. "You are a life saver," Willa announced before stretching up and leaving a kiss on Cassidy's cheek.

Cassidy cringed and wiped the lipstick mark off her face with the back of her hand before Willa took off in a hurry, out the double doors of the basketball court.

Chapter Twenty-seven

Willa came to a halt outside of the front desk area so that she could straighten out her summer dress and run her fingers through the length of her hair before opening the door to the office. Brynn looked up as she entered, but Willa could tell by her bewildered look that she hadn't expected her to be the one to walk in.

Cassidy had been right; Brynn didn't appear to be her usual tough self. She sat low in her wheelchair and an air of exhaustion loomed over her. She looked as though she didn't sleep at all the previous night. Willa knew that when Brynn shifted to a more upright position, and flashed a cordial smile, that it was a fake show for pride's sake.

"After you left, I realized that I probably made it seem like I had used you for some sort of entertainment for myself. I can't even imagine how that must have made you feel. I've been ashamed of myself for that since you left last night," Brynn rambled off rapidly. She might have continued on, but Willa approached her and laid a soft kiss on her lips and then pulled back to stare warmly at her face.

"You did absolutely nothing wrong. We both shared a wonderful moment that made me feel so amazing. It was my own self-conscious mind that made more out of it than I should have, and now I want to make up for it by showing you the same attention back."

Brynn's eyes narrowed as she searched her face, but Willa wasn't going to give up any answers so easily. Willa's plan was one that Brynn needed to experience, not discuss. She started by flipping up the brakes on the wheelchair. Brynn's fingers twitched and she reached to take control of the wheels. Willa could see that she was masking the distress of not being in control, so she swiftly guided her through the doorway into the bathroom, before she could change her mind. Working quickly, she locked the door behind them, then slipped out of her dress, bra, and underwear, carelessly tossing the articles of clothing aside on the floor.

Brynn's eyes were locked onto Willa, as she used her own body as a distraction to make Brynn feel more at ease with what was to come. Willa took each of Brynn's hands and leaned down to place them on each one of her breasts while she stole a long kiss from her lips. When she was satisfied that Brynn was more relaxed than before, she reached down to the bottom of her shirt to raise it up, exposing her stomach.

The expected immediate response to stop her came when the warmth of Brynn's hand left Willa's breast and pushed her shirt back down. "I can't," Brynn insisted.

Willa took Brynn's hands in hers and demanded her attention with her eyes. "I know you won't admit that this scares the hell out of you, please understand that it does me too, but I'd like you to trust me enough to let me try something with you."

Willa could feel the tremors of unease shake below the surface of Brynn's skin, but still, she gave her consent with a nod of her head. With her permission, Willa was able to remove her shirt and sports bra with ease. She would have liked to spend some time giving attention to the perfectly shaped breasts that she released, but she knew there was a time frame that she had to work with in order to gain Brynn's trust in her. She moved on to sliding her shorts and underwear off with the help of Brynn lifting her body weight up off her legs.

Before Brynn could protest, she guided her through the doorway of the shower and tapped her hand on the seat in the center. Brynn followed her visual instruction to move onto the seat and Willa pushed her empty wheelchair back out and closed the shower door.

A startled look swept over Brynn's face over the separation of what was essentially an extension of her own body. Willa realized that when Brynn was alone in the shower, she must have her chair within reach of herself, and to see it so far away must've been terrifying. "I'm here," she assured her with a fleeting kiss on her way to the shower faucets. She averted the showerheads until the temperature was comfortable, and then eased them to a low pressure so that a gentle mist sprayed them both.

When she looked to Brynn to see if the atmosphere was acceptable to her, she noticed that she was being perused with an unrelenting lust. Willa decided to turn the act of tying her hair up into a little show for Brynn as she swayed her hips while swooping her long blonde curls up into a manageable cluster at the back of her head and into a hair tie. When she got close enough for Brynn to reach out for her, a pair of strong hands pulled her near, in a ravenous need to touch her.

As much as Willa wanted to explore the body that she had finally uncovered, this was also about pleasing

Brynn and if she desired Willa, then she wouldn't deny her that pleasure. Willa lifted one of her long legs up and placed her foot on the tiled armrest. She reached between her legs, situated a finger along either side of her clit so that it was fully exposed and used her other hand to guide Brynn's mouth directly on it.

After a few minutes, Willa was fighting with herself to stay upright for as long as she could. She wanted to melt into Brynn's arms, but she didn't dare move, yearning not to break away from the pulsing of Brynn's tongue against her. As if Brynn was reading her mind, Brynn lifted Willa's raised leg and took on the weight of it over her shoulder, making it easier to balance.

Willa took advantage of the new position to rub her hands the length of Brynn's neck. Her fingers dug into the hard muscles with a matching motion of Brynn's fingers sliding in and out of her. When her body shook with her orgasm, she moved down to straddle Brynn's lap and held Brynn's head tightly to her chest. The comfort of pressing her face against the top of Brynn's head while running her fingers through her short hair had a calming sensation that she had spent years searching for in objects and now found in a person. Brynn had always been the solid foundation that kept her grounded and it felt good to have her back again.

Willa cupped Brynn's face in her hands and lifted it so that she could look into the hauntingly bright blue eyes that made her skin ripple out in goose bumps despite the warm water beading down on them. "I think it's safe to assume that there's enough water coming down on us that if you needed to, we wouldn't even notice if an accident were to occur, right?"

Brynn closed her eyes and let out a shaky breath before opening them again. A quiet, "Yeah," was all that came out.

Willa kissed her while dropping one hand down to circle Brynn's nipple with her finger. When she glanced down to witness the hard point that she had created, she smiled at the stark contrast of her light skin against the dark bronze of Brynn's skin. She stepped down to the floor of the shower and carefully lifted each one of Brynn's legs to separate them. Brynn's face feigned a slight smile, but Willa could tell that she was covering up for the insecurity of her legs, thin and lacking muscle from years of not being able to use them. Willa made a point of caressing the length of them sensually with her gaze to show that she thought they were equally as beautiful as the rest of her.

She knelt down and drew Brynn's attention back to her by gliding her thumb across the surface of her labia. She enjoyed watching the transition of Brynn's body as it went from an on-guard position to a relaxed state when she leaned back in the tiled seat, allowing Willa to have complete control of her.

Willa took her time in the details of every part of her. She played at one nipple with her tongue while twirling her fingertips around the other one, tugging at it until Brynn moaned with pleasure. She kissed her way down her stomach, into every curve of her perfect ab muscles and then dipped her tongue down further to where Brynn was already intensely sensitive to every slight touch that she offered. Despite wanting to spend some time going slowly on Brynn's clit, Willa sensed an urgency in her, a need for Willa to give her what she had been wanting for so long. Brynn's clit was already swollen and ready for the attention that she yearned for. Willa covered it with the width of her tongue and smiled when she heard the faint whimper escape from Brynn's mouth. She then slid two fingers into Brynn and used the tip of her thumb to gently massage the space below her clit, while simultaneously slipping in and out of her. The sensation of all three motions at the same time had Brynn clenching around her fingers with tiny contractions within minutes.

Brynn's fingers spread out over the tiles on either side of her as she allowed the orgasm to take over her. When Willa's fingers slid out of her, the length of her tongue immediately replaced them for the last few moments of pleasure to be shared in the most intimate way possible.

When Willa felt Brynn's body settle into a motionless state, she left one final caress with her lips and moved back far enough to take in the sight of the exquisite woman in front of her. She couldn't help but stare in awe at the strongest woman she had ever known, reduced to a blissfully vulnerable status. Willa climbed up into the seat next to Brynn, snuggled up against her, and they entwined their bodies together, kissing until the shower water wrinkled their fingertips.

After they were dried off and dressed, Willa stole Griffin's oversized leather office chair from behind his desk and moved it to Brynn's corner of the office, where she lounged with her legs up on the desk. Brynn was situated facing her with a hand caressing Willa's leg. Every so often, her fingertips would wander high up under Willa's dress.

"Cut that out," Willa scolded her. "Cass might come in here and I've been yelled at by her enough for one day."

"Again? You seriously need to let me have a talk

with her."

"No, she's just very protective of you and it's understandable. She's afraid that when I leave, I'm going to hurt you all over again."

Brynn's eyes shifted to the wheel on her chair, which she prodded at with her thumb. "Laurel Cove can't offer you the glamorous lifestyle that you've created for yourself and I understand that. I'm not naïve; I know you'll have to leave eventually."

Willa reached for the bottom of Brynn's shirt and filled her fist with as much of the fabric as she could bunch up, trying to hold onto something solid as her mind swirled. "Tomorrow, actually. I'm leaving tomorrow."

"Oh." Brynn swallowed hard and cleared her throat. "What about your dad's house? I thought you were putting it on the market before you leave."

"That was the plan, but because I ended up doing everything other than preparing it for sale, I ran out of time. Before coming here, I had an entire book tour scheduled that I thought that I might have to postpone, but as of this morning, my publisher informed me that she didn't cancel any of the events."

"So, are you keeping the house?"

"No, Aunt Beth is going to put the remaining items in storage and sell the house for me, since the process is too emotional for me to deal with. I think it'll be easier for me this way."

Brynn brushed the back of her knuckles down Willa's calf muscle. "Let Beth know that if she needs any help, I can box stuff up for her. Griff can do the heavy lifting and use his truck for the big furniture items."

Willa could feel a tremble in Brynn's touch and

see a lost look in her eyes.

"At the end of summer, I'll be done with most of my projects and I can come back." She leaned forward, kissed the side of Brynn's neck, and nuzzled her face into it. "I promise I'll come back."

Brynn raked her fingers through Willa's hair. "I know you will," she whispered into her ear.

"Can we maybe have dinner together tonight?" Willa asked.

"I'd love to, but Griffin will be back from his trip any time now. I have to meet him at the house and, as you know, we have a lot to discuss."

Willa sighed and wrapped her arms around Brynn. "In that case, I better hold onto you now, so that I can carry a good memory of you in my heart while I'm away."

Chapter Twenty-eight

Willa was surprised to see both Shannon and Megan out on the deck of The Anchor when she arrived after leaving the fitness center.

"I had to take the shift off so that I could have a farewell drink with you before you left the Cove," Shannon said, pouring a glass of Willa's favorite wine.

Willa took a seat and placed a hand on top of each of theirs. "I can't even thank the both of you enough for helping me through one of the most difficult times of my life. It was truly a blessing to have found a friendship with you ladies."

"We are only a phone call away if you need to talk, medical questions or anything else you need," Shannon assured her.

"Thank you, Dr. Martin," Willa teased.

Megan tried to fan away the moisture forming around her eyes. "Please tell me we won't have to wait until our fortieth reunion until we see you again?"

"Are you kidding me? Every free moment I have, I'll be driving up the coast to decompress at the Cove. Especially after the day I just had…" Willa unsuccessfully tried to cover up the blush creeping up on her cheeks by taking a sip of her wine.

"The talk went well then?" Shannon asked.

"Talk? It appears as though a lot more than just talking took place," Megan blurted out.

Shannon's eyes widened and Willa almost choked

on her drink.

"Well, now you know the other reason why you'll be seeing a bit more of me around here, every opportunity I can get."

"I'm glad that you got everything straightened out after our conversation this morning."

"Yes, we overcame a huge obstacle today, although there's still so much that I have to learn about Brynn. It's impossible to get her to open up to me about certain things, especially medically."

"Like I said before, the offer is still there to mediate a conversation between the two of you. I can fill in for Brynn when she has difficulty describing the more technical terms for her injury. Maybe it's something that I can convince Brynn into doing when she has her next appointment."

"That would be helpful, since she tends to hide certain things, even from herself, it seems. It hurts me to find sharps containers filled with used syringes hidden in the cabinets."

Shannon set her glass down and unfolded her legs. The other women watched as the doctor struggled to work through something on her mind.

"I shouldn't have brought that up. I know you can't discuss patient information with us." Willa tried to end the subject that was causing discomfort to Shannon.

Shannon raised her hand. "No, I'm just trying to figure out if it's safe to say when something has nothing to do with a patient."

Megan looked back and forth between her equally confused friends. "Kind of like the situation in which you told Willa that she wasn't to blame for Griffin not going to college?"

Shannon pointed to Megan in triumph. "Exactly!"

"Okay, so what Shannon's trying to tell us but can't is that Brynn doesn't need needles for a prescribed medication."

"But I found them at both the gym and at her house. If she's not taking anything..."

"They must belong to Griffin!" Megan concluded.

Shannon put both her hands up in the air and shook her head. "He's technically not my patient, but he was one at the clinic before my time. Everything I learned was through past records through the clinic. Not that I could confirm anything either way."

"Willa and I found out yesterday about his steroid use in high school, so that's not a secret anymore."

Willa sat on the edge of her seat. "Is it possible that he might still be using steroids?"

Shannon's face contorted with unease. "Please don't ask me to diagnose him on the basis of rumors. I am currently treading on very dangerous territory with my career right now."

Willa took a hold of Shannon's wrist and looked her in the eyes. "You told me not to believe the rumors about him because you knew about his history of steroid use. As a doctor, you must know the signs and symptoms of current use. Do you suspect in any way that he might still be using?" Willa clenched her jaw and raised her hand up to stop Shannon from needing to respond. "I know, you can't answer that, but for Brynn's sake, please tell me if he could possibly be a danger to his sister if she were to provoke him in some way to make him very angry."

Shannon nodded and Willa stood up, nearly knocking her chair over behind her. Both Megan and Shannon yelled out her name after her, but she was already rounding the corner of the building and she did not intend to use up vital time to go back and explain to them that she had to check on Brynn.

Willa parked her car behind Griffin's truck and raced up the walkway to the front porch. For the first time since she had been back, she didn't hesitate to knock on the door. After a couple of polite knocks without a response, she resorted to a pounding of her fist against the thick storm door. When that got her no results, she took a deep breath and turned the handle.

The entryway, living room, and kitchen were all vacant and even a quick scan of the back patio showed no signs of either of the Reed twins. Willa paused for a moment and listened as she heard the muffled sound of angry voices coming from down the hall. She made her way towards the sound, but slower and more cautiously than she had been moving around before.

Brynn's bedroom and the bathroom were both empty so Willa continued on to the next bedroom, which she assumed belonged to Griffin. She angled her head enough to see what was happening without catching the attention of either one of them. A large opened suitcase was spread out on the bed; a mess of clothes was overflowing out of it. Brynn had somehow cornered her brother in the space between his bed, nightstand, and the wall. She glared at him while yelling out accusations of lying to her about both the time she was in the hospital and about college.

Willa couldn't help but to be reminded of when they were young and she witnessed them getting into screaming matches with one another over random sibling problems. Many of the arguments that Mrs. Reed didn't intercept resulted in a physical match of strength as they wrestled it out, until exhaustion or injury left one of them victorious. There had been many times when Brynn wouldn't back down no matter how intensely Griffin would push her to the limit of what her body could handle. She would take every jab that he had to offer with a smile on her face and go back for more, often times pummeling him to the ground to end it. It was afterwards that Willa would catch Brynn nursing a wound or bruise in private where no one would see her in pain. Sometimes Willa would let Brynn have her moment alone to compose herself and join them again to return to their fun. There were other times, though, when Willa felt the need to comfort her with a hug to show that she understood that the true strength Brynn had was not to show weakness in front of her brother.

There was no sign of that weakness even now, as Brynn berated Griffin with verbal blows. She threw insults at him one after another, leaving no time in between for him to answer for himself.

Griffin's broad shoulders were hunched forward and his glassy eyes never left the view of the floor as he absorbed every claim that Brynn made about his past. It was clear that Brynn wouldn't allow him the opportunity to speak until she had spilled out every thought that she had trapped in her mind. Afterwards, a silence filled the room, but he either didn't notice, or didn't know if he should speak.

Brynn's body was stiff and shaking with rage as her chest puffed out as high as she could sit, angled up towards Griffin. Willa knew that if Brynn could, she would be right up in his face, antagonizing him until he acknowledged her.

"So, is it fucking true or not?" Brynn demanded to know.

"Who told you these things?"

"It doesn't matter how I found out; what matters is whether you did them or not."

"It was Willa. She came back here and filled your head with a bunch of bullshit and you believe everything she says."

Willa silently gasped at the sound of Griffin spitting out her name as if she was the source of all their problems. The pit of her stomach shook with fear and anxiety but she kept her feet planted to the spot, not wanting to flee from Brynn when a hidden danger lurked within Griffin's body, ready to explode at any time.

"Don't blame anyone else for your actions, especially Willa. She's as much a victim of your lies as I am."

Griffin's eyes narrowed as he scrutinized Brynn. "The only reason you would defend Willa is that you've been with her."

"Does it still make you jealous that she would choose me over you?"

"If she wants you now, it's only because she feels sorry for what she did to you."

Willa caught the change in Brynn's expression, which first swept over with an undeniable sadness. She wanted then to pull Brynn aside, kiss her, embrace her, and tell her repeatedly that pity was not the reason why she made love to her.

Willa's chest tightened with an ache that yearned to console Brynn for the wedge that Griffin was attempting to place between them. Thankfully, it didn't take long for Brynn to recognize his deceit and she shifted back into an agitated state.

"Tell me, Griff, what hurts you more? That you

can't scam me out of every cent I earn anymore, that your best friend leaked to the entire town that you have a steroid addiction, or that I'm sleeping with the only woman that you ever really cared about?"

"Oh no," Willa whispered inaudibly under her breath. She wanted Brynn to stand up for herself and not to fall for his deceptions, but it was another thing for her to taunt him.

The list of accusations was the trigger that flipped the internal switch of Griffin's mood from seething to irate. With absolutely no indication that he was about to attack, Griffin lunged at Brynn, pushing hard against her chest with one hand while wrapping his other around her throat to choke her.

It was one thing for them to have fighting matches as children, but for Griffin to brutally attack his adult sister was an entirely different situation, and Willa would not allow the abuse to continue.

Griffin yelled a streaming flow of obscenities at the top of his lungs. The bellowing noise provided enough cover for her to make an entrance into the room unnoticed. She didn't hesitate to bound across the bed and fling her upper body so that she was creating a wall across Griffin's outstretched arms and Brynn's face.

The abrupt approach startled Griffin enough that his hand slipped down from Brynn's neck, but he maintained a hold of the fabric on the collar of her T-shirt. Willa found her face a mere few inches from Griffin's. He grinned a malicious smile and a sickening wave shot through Willa. She realized that because she wasn't any real threat to him physically, he didn't care about backing down.

Willa should have been afraid. When she saw the lack of emotion in his eyes, she should have backed away. When she noticed the void of humanity in the low growl he emitted as he bellowed her name, she should have run for her life. None of those things mattered, though, because she was taking his focus away from Brynn and any amount of protection she could offer was her only goal.

She hadn't planned on her next move, let alone what to possibly say to him, but she didn't have to, because before she could recognize what was happening to her, Willa was being raised up into the air. Two other arms tried their best to keep Willa grounded, but strength and height won out and the safety of the anchor below her became untethered. She had no control of her own body as Griffin easily tossed her aside like a toddler throwing a doll.

The room seemed to spin until Willa figured out that she was spinning as she plummeted down into the narrow space between the wall and Brynn's wheelchair. She recognized the loud crack as her head hit the windowsill on the way down. For a split second, she felt the uncomfortable sensation of being trapped with her face wedged against the metal rim of the large wheel, but it didn't last long because the darkness set in quickly.

Chapter Twenty-nine

*W*illa awoke into the same familiar setting. She was once again at the graduation party by the pool, with Brynn standing in front of her. The repetitive scenario played itself out the same exact way that it always had, except this time, Willa allowed herself to be more present in the recollection of the moments.

When Brynn's lips pressed up against hers, she granted herself permission to embrace the emotions of her past. What she found hidden within the recesses of her mind was the sensation of pure love for her friend, newly emerged with the first fleeting kiss between them.

After the revelation of how she truly felt, everything in the dream changed, as if Willa was experiencing it for the first time.

When the kiss ended, and she opened her eyes, she saw that look of pure rage on Griffin's face. Willa had always believed that he meant his rage for her, that he was so angry with her for her betrayal of their relationship. What she noticed this time was that his focus was on Brynn. That same malicious grin that he had shown to Willa had been directed towards his own sister all those years ago.

Willa watched, as if trapped in a sickening playback, as Griffin wound back his arm with perfect pitcher's form and aimed the baseball that he had been tossing in the air directly at the back of Brynn's head.

She knew now how it had been so instinctual for

her to use her own body as a human shield between the two Reed twins in the midst of a verbal argument that had turned to blows, because it wasn't the first time that she had done it.

The pool was supposed to be the safe option. She could send Brynn to the one place that she would have a wet, but otherwise unharmed landing, away from the projectile rapidly approaching her head. All she had to do was push her hard enough to make sure that she lost her balance and fell in.

What she didn't account for was that Brynn had enough alcohol in her system for her normally skillful reaction time to be reduced to next to nothing. She also didn't know that because of that, her body would fall backwards and hit the concrete edge of the pool before falling in and hitting her neck against the wall of it under the water.

Anything was better in Willa's mind compared to a baseball to the back of the skull. Despite the horrified look on Brynn's face as she pushed her, Willa was confident that she had made the right decision. She didn't even regret her choice as the ball missed its intended target and collided with the side of her head.

Just as it had done so only moments ago when she was awake, darkness once more consumed Willa.

Opening her eyes took all the energy that she had, but Willa could tell by the sounds in the room that things were not resolved yet, and Brynn could still be in danger. She raised herself up onto her hands and knees, trying to focus on where everyone had moved to, because she was no longer wedged between the wall and a wheel.

Griffin had pushed Brynn back with his forearm to her neck, so that she had rolled up against the bureau in the corner of the room. By the time Willa had used the bedpost to hoist herself up from the floor, their upper limbs were entwined in a battle of swinging and blocking punches, but Brynn was taking the brunt of them because she was unable to dodge out of the way like Griffin could.

Willa wavered unsteadily, still dizzy from being knocked unconscious, and unable to shake the ringing noise from her ears from the impact of the windowsill. She pressed the palm of her hand to the spot on her head that hurt more than the other areas, and a wave of nausea swept through her. The mattress that she was leaning against looked inviting, but the sickening sounds of two people pummeling each other across the room snapped her out of the daze that she was falling into.

After a particularly powerful punch that Brynn took in the ribs, she leaned forward and clutched at her stomach. Willa watched in horror as Griffin retracted his fist in preparation for the next big hit that looked to be aimed at her face. Willa flung herself at Griffin's back and clutched her hands up around his arm, pulling it to her chest. Griffin could have easily tugged it from her weak grasp, but something about the way she was holding him made him pause in mid attack.

Instead of struggling with Griffin or fighting him off long enough for Brynn to recover and join in, she clutched onto him in an awkward embrace with her forehead pressed into his shoulder. He glared down at her, and Willa readied herself to become the next target of his fury, but something changed in him as she stared up at him through her tangled mess of hair and let herself crumple up against his arm.

"I'm so sorry that I hurt you, Griff," Willa

mumbled into his arm, through trembling lips.

Brynn raised her head up from her hunched over position and squinted her eyes at Willa, looking bewildered. "That's a pretty bad concussion you got, huh?"

Willa shook her head in protest. "You hurt him too, Brynn. That's why he's so angry at both of us." She looked up into Griff's eyes, the same shade of blue as Brynn's. "I remember everything from that night now."

Griffin tried to back away from her, like a frightened animal, but she clung to him anyway. "How?" he asked.

"Must have been the knock to my head that jogged my memory back into me. Kind of like the hit I took to the head from the baseball you threw that night." Willa looked over at Brynn to make sure that she was paying close attention. "The one intended to hit you."

Brynn's nostrils flared and she gritted her teeth. She looked prepared to take him on for another round, regardless of the condition she was currently in. "If he tried to hurt or possibly kill me that night, then why are you apologizing to him?"

"Because I genuinely believe that he was hurt when he saw you kiss me. You betrayed your own brother and it must have broken his heart to see us making out in front of him and his friends, especially on a night when he probably already knew that he wasn't going to be heading off to college like the rest of us." Willa looked back up at Griffin. "You were already addicted to using the steroids at that point, weren't you?"

Griffin nodded, his face scrunched up like a child

caught doing something wrong.

"It's not an excuse for what he did, though," Brynn said, her voice still raised with mixed emotions.

"No, it's not, but all three of us did things that night and afterwards that led up to *this*." Willa waved her hands around, motioning towards her head, Brynn's split lip, and Griffin's swollen eye.

Both Brynn and Griffin averted their eyes down to the floor. She knew that they must both be embarrassed to have her reprimanding them.

"Sorry, bro. If I'd known you had a problem, you know I would have had your back."

"It's okay, sis. I just wish you weren't in that chair because of me."

"Nah, it's my fault for kissing your girl."

"We both know that she always liked you better, anyway," Griffin admitted.

Griffin and Brynn shared a sly look between themselves. Willa was glad that something as simple as their shared feelings towards her, and the way they could still joke about it, showed the true camaraderie linking the siblings together.

"While I'm glad that you two are back to being civil with one another, I'd like to be the judge of my own feelings, if you don't mind," Willa said, folding her arms across her chest. When she realized that they were both staring in wait for her admission, she became self-conscious of her disheveled appearance. After patting down a wrinkled part of her outfit and flipping some of her hair back over her ear, she coolly added, "I find you both equally charming, but yes, I prefer the companionship of a woman."

Brynn smirked and shot a wink in her brother's direction.

Willa sighed, knowing there were still so many more steps that needed to be taken for the healing process between the three of them, but she was thankful that things didn't end as badly as it could have.

Her shoes had flown off her feet during the commotion and Willa bent down to retrieve them, but the woozy rush of dizziness flooded her on the way down. Griffin noticed her uneasiness and swiftly scooped her up before she went down. He lifted her as if she weighed nothing and set her down in Brynn's outstretched arms.

Brynn pulled Willa into a gentle but firm embrace as she cradled her in her arms. "We should call Dr. Martin and have her come take a look at you."

Willa shook her head to protest, but she closed her eyes when the motion made the room spin. She pressed her palm to her head and winced. "I think you're right."

Griffin gave Willa's arm a little squeeze to show his thanks and then he sank down to the floor in front of them. He placed one hand on Willa's knee and the other on Brynn's arm. "I'm so sorry. I need help, but I don't know how or what to do."

"I'll help you with whatever it takes to get you better. We can get you into the best rehabilitation center in the country. I have lots of contacts in the industry that can help us out with this process."

"Why would you do all of this for me after what I've done to hurt you?"

"Because I know the kind, caring, and compassionate man that you can be when the drugs aren't controlling you. You took care of my father and Brynn for all those years when I abandoned them both and for that, I owe you the world."

A few minutes later, Willa snuggled up to Brynn in her bed where Griffin had placed her before heading off to fetch them some pain medication and water. Brynn winced when Willa wrapped her arm around her. She looked at her, concerned. "Maybe we should get you looked at; there could be some broken ribs in here," she said, gliding her fingertips over the surface of Brynn's skin.

"Nah, I've taken worse hits than this falling out of my chair playing basketball. I'll survive after some sessions with the ice pack."

Willa moved her thumb up to the corner of Brynn's lip and wiped away a drip of blood that had formed there from the split skin. "And will some ice fix this, too?"

"That might need something else."

"Oh yeah, like what?"

"A kiss, for starters."

"Hmm, well, I'll give you that, but I don't know if I have anything else to offer you right now," Willa said wearily. She guided the side of Brynn's face with her hand so that she could reach her lips. She left a row of delicate little kisses along the bruised skin on her cheek and the corner of her mouth where the cut was. She could taste the copper flavor of the blood on her tongue and the salt from her perspiration.

"The kiss will do," Brynn whispered into her mouth.

Chapter Thirty

After nearly two months of being shuffled from city to city around the world, promoting her latest book as well as her latest movie release, Willa finally crossed the bridge that led to Laurel Cove. A seagull swooped in low enough to almost touch the hood of her car and then glided off towards the water, landing on a wooden pillar protruding from the rocky coastline. She rolled her window down so that she could take her first breath of fresh air and inhale the scent of the pine trees lining the sides of the road.

A large pickup truck approached her on the opposite side of the road, and she moved over on the narrow strip of pavement so that they could both pass simultaneously. The driver of the truck tipped the brim of his sun faded ball cap in gratitude as he passed and Willa nodded in return. It was the small things like that which made the tiny island community so intimate compared to most other towns, or any city for that matter.

Rounding the bend and passing by her father's house with the *sold* sign covering the top of the realtor agency sign left a pang of sadness in her heart. She hoped that the new owners might let her stop by for tea every now and then. Willa continued towards the waterfront, where she pulled into the marina parking lot and hurried down the dock to where *The Elaine* was waiting.

"Miss Barton, the winds are calm for you today," Blake greeted her as she approached the boat.

"Thank you for letting us borrow her for a couple of hours," she said, tossing her bag onto the deck before getting in herself.

"Aye, she's all yours, my dear." Blake untied the rope that attached the boat to the dock and handed it over to Willa.

Griffin meandered out of the cabin, standing as tall and strong as ever before, but he had a calm demeanor about him that was different. Willa took a couple of steps in his direction and he picked her up off her feet into a giant bear hug. "Did you forget to tell your wardrobe director that you were going to be on a boat today?" he joked, referring to her designer suit and heels.

She furrowed her brow and pouted her lips. "I'll have you know that I dress myself, but I had a meeting this morning before I left and didn't have time to change."

"Ah, I'm just messing with you," he said, running a hand through his cropped black hair.

Willa looked up at Griffin through squinted eyes. His massive height made him difficult to see with the sun glaring right behind his head. "Are you doing as well as you look?"

He dipped his head down and scratched at the back of his neck. "It was rough going, at first, but thanks to all the help you've gotten me, I'm on the right track."

Willa smiled warmly at all the effort that he had put into his rehabilitation program to help with his steroid addiction. She had funded it, but he took a great initiative at completing it and even staying longer than required when he admitted that he wasn't ready to leave yet. He also proudly informed her that he had signed up for classes to get a coaching certificate, which couldn't have made Willa any happier for him. She had all the faith in the world that he had turned his life around.

"Please don't hesitate to ask if you need anything at all. I'm here for you, always."

"The same goes for me."

"Thanks, Griff."

She turned towards the cabin area where Brynn was, but a hand on her arm held her back from heading to the front of the boat. "Give her a minute or two. She's saying her goodbyes now. You know she doesn't like people seeing her get all emotional over anything."

Willa leaned against the side of the boat and watched Brynn from a distance. She was holding the silver urn in her hands and having a whispered conversation with it. Her hand came up and swiped at the tears that trickled down her cheeks. Willa wanted so badly to comfort her, but Griffin was right; Brynn would be too embarrassed share in her grief.

Willa busied herself with watching the little waves of water splash up against the sides of the boat in a steady rhythm, which helped to settle her hectic lifestyle into the slower paced setting of life in Maine. She didn't even notice that Brynn was beside her until she felt a hand on her lower back.

The giant smile that spread across her face made the perfect cover up for the anguish that Willa knew overcame Brynn moments earlier. She wanted to caress Brynn's cheek and convince her that it's okay to shed some tears over the loss of a man that they both considered a father. She yearned to have the strong woman before her be just a little unguarded, so that she could take over the role of protector for once, but Brynn wouldn't want that, and so Willa allowed her to hide behind the glowing smile.

There was a hesitation between both women, not sure of how to go about a greeting after eight weeks of separation with only a random phone call between them every now and again. Griffin had to have noticed the awkwardness in the air, because he bowed out and made his way to the front of the boat. Willa assumed that he, too, would take a private period of time to mourn, while they were busy getting reacquainted, but the motor started up immediately and he busied himself with navigating out of the harbor.

When the boat picked up a little momentum in the open water, Brynn situated herself into a corner of the deck and set her brakes. Willa figured that she probably used to go on fishing trips with her father many times over the years, based on the familiarity of the spot she settled into. There were stories of adventures between the two people that she loved so dearly that she wanted to hear about someday, but there would be plenty of time for those in the future.

Willa approached her shyly, wanting to make a physical connection with her, but not sure how to go about doing it. When she got close enough, though, Brynn took over by practically scooping Willa into her lap. She let out a loud gasp at the unexpected loss of her footing, but the whirring of the motor drowned out the sound.

Willa dipped her face in close to Brynn's, thinking that they would kiss, being so close to one another, but Brynn wasn't even making eye contact with her. Willa watched as she curiously used her fingers to push aside the outer layer of her suit jacket and explore the inner dress shirt collar that was made from a billowing white silk material.

"Go ahead and make your wisecrack comment about my choice of attire for our boat ride. Your brother already gave his opinion about it."

"It doesn't matter to me what you want to wear."

"Then why are you so concerned with checking out how many layers I've got on?"

"I'm planning ahead to see how much work I'll have in order to take all this off you later."

Brynn's eyebrows raised with the question of whether Willa also wanted the same outcome for later in the night as she did. Willa couldn't form the words quickly enough to give the answer she wanted to convey, so instead she offered the kiss that she so desperately wanted as her reply. When their lips finally separated, Brynn flashed a captivating wink and Willa understood that she received the acknowledgement loud and clear. With the anticipation of much more to come later that night, they silently made a mutual agreement to keep the overtly affectionate displays to a minimum around Griffin, out of respect.

It took a lot less time than Willa thought it would to get out far enough from the Cove to be in open water, where not a single parcel of land could be seen. She figured the time ticked away swiftly because of the inevitable goodbye that awaited her at the end of the journey. Griffin decreased the speed of the motor on the boat and it slowed to a gentle hum before he cut the power to it completely, leaving just the sounds of the sea to fill the quiet that no one dared to break.

The urn weighed heavy in Willa's hands as she held it out over the side of the boat. There were so many things that she had prepared to say prior to this day, but at the last minute the only words that managed to escape her mouth were "Goodbye, Dad."

They all laid a hand on the urn and helped to tip it so that his ashes would scatter on the surface of the water. She took the photo that her father had taped to his boat of the three of them, stuck it inside the urn, and tossed it overboard with his remains.

Willa hung her head over the side of the boat and kept watch until every speck of dust that was visible on the tiny rippling waves was either pulled under or swept too far out of sight for her to see. By that time, most of the tears she had shed were dried up and the rest that fell were wiped away with Brynn's thumb as they made their way back to shore.

The boat approached a dock in Laurel Cove, but it wasn't the same one they had left earlier. Willa and Griffin exchanged knowing glances, but Brynn looked thoroughly confused.

"What's going on?" Brynn asked.

"You'll see," Willa said whimsically as she tossed her bag over onto the dock.

Griffin lifted Brynn into his arms and waited on the dock while Willa transported her wheelchair over as well. Brynn had no choice but to go along with their secret plan but Willa could see that she was starting to get antsy when Griffin got back in the boat, so Willa waved him off after untying the rope that anchored it to the dock.

"How about a little explanation as to why we were dropped off behind the old stone house you were always obsessed with?"

"The answer is in a story that I'll tell you on our way up to the house," Willa explained, motioning towards the ramp at the end of the dock.

Willa knew that Brynn would have liked her to go first, but when she didn't budge, Brynn finally gave in and headed toward the house. "We're moving, so start talking," she said over her shoulder.

"My *obsession*, as you call it, with this house, began with us dreaming about living here someday when we were kids."

"I remember you wanted to read books up in that tower, and I wanted to climb up the outside of it."

They reached the gigantic back deck of the house and Willa ran up the ramp that led to it. Brynn watched her, wide eyed, but followed her cautiously to the top. Willa watched carefully as Brynn examined the boards below her as she went up the ramp.

Willa sucked in a breath of the fresh sea breeze and spun in a circle, letting her hair flow out in a mess of curls around her face. "It's absolutely gorgeous back here, isn't it?" she asked with a delighted laugh.

Brynn smiled at Willa's joyful display, but she kept a cautious eye out on her surroundings. "It's nice, but it's still summer. Don't you think the owners might catch us out here?"

Willa made a show of pretending to sneak up to the sliding glass door before she slid it open and stepped in. "I thought you used to be the daring one," Willa said, sticking her head back out the door, willing Brynn to follow her.

Brynn found Willa lounging in a room that overlooked the view of the ocean. Her feet were up on the coffee table and her arms were spread wide across the top of the couch cushions.

"I'm guessing there's more to the story that you still haven't finished?"

"My mother's estranged parents, who owned this as a summer home, passed away a year apart from each other, and with my deceased mother as their only child, the house was left to my father and in turn to me. I found the deed in with Dad's paperwork while I was cleaning up his estate."

"Are you going to sell it?"

"I'd planned on that initially, but then I decided to hire a construction crew to come in and make some changes to the house."

"What kind of changes?"

Willa got up and made her way through the house with Brynn close behind. "As you can see, all of the doorways have been enlarged so that they are wider." She then moved past a bathroom and pointed in. "The showers have been renovated just like the large one in the office bathroom at the gym." Willa walked up to a door at the base of the staircase. "I had an elevator installed which goes to the second floor." Willa stopped explaining the remodeling details when they reached the kitchen.

Brynn approached the counters, where all of them were custom made to be low enough for her to reach them, as well as the sink and stovetop. She reached out and touched her fingertips to the knobs on the back of the stove. For a long time, she didn't move, but a shaking motion in her shoulders made Willa go to her. She crouched down in front of Brynn and kissed every one of her knuckles until the tremors subsided.

"I talked to Griffin and he thinks that it would be best for his recovery if the two of you had a little space for a while."

"So, you fixed up this house for me to be able to live here?"

"Yes, unless you don't like it, and in that case, I could have it all put back and Griff could move in."

"No, Willa, it's perfect. I never imagined a place that was suited for all my needs could exist. I don't know how to thank you enough for this."

"Well, there is something…"

Brynn pushed back the hair that had fallen into Willa's face. "Anything for you."

"Well, I did sell a house this week, but it was my condo in New York."

"Seriously? Does that mean you're going to stay here?"

"Mm-hmm. I can work from anywhere, really, and what better place than Laurel Cove, right?" Willa bit at her lower lip. "That is, if you don't mind a roommate?"

Brynn crinkled up her nose. "I'm not so sure about that."

Willa sunk down further onto the tiled floor, trying to hide a sullen face. "Oh, it's okay. I'm sure I could look into renting a room at the Sea Turtle Inn for a few nights until I find a new place…"

Brynn's lips twisted up into her famous smirk. "Do you honestly believe that I would ever allow you to sleep anywhere on this island other than in my arms?"

"But you just said that you didn't want a roommate."

"I don't. I've had Griff for a roommate for the past twenty years." Brynn leaned her face down and put her lips to Willa's ear. "It's about time I have a lover." She kissed her earlobe. "Or a girlfriend." She kissed her cheek. "Or a wife." She kissed her lips.

Willa closed her eyes and let the kiss linger on her lips. "It's about time I have those things too."

About the Author

Sarah Turtle spent the beginning portion of her childhood living in a small Maine island community, much like the setting in her debut novel, Laurel Cove. She moved around to other locations far from the East Coast, such as San Diego, but eventually came back to live in her home state of Maine. She just couldn't imagine not being able to enjoy the rocky coastline of New England, or the cold winter blizzards that she loves more than anything.

When she's not busy writing, Sarah loves going on bike rides, playing board games, video games, painting, and playing a variety of musical instruments. Faithfully by her side in all things, is her Jack Russell Terrier dog, Guinn.

Facebook - SarahTurtleAuthor
Twitter - @writergrrl78

Other books by Sapphire Authors

Highland Dew – ISBN – 978-1-948232-11-1

Bryce Andrews, west coast sales director for Global Distillers and Distribution, is tired of the corporate hamster wheel. She needs a change.

A craft whisky trade show offers her inspiration and a chance to revisit Scotland and the majestic scenery of the Speyside region—best known for the "Whisky Trail." Bryce and her coworker, Reggie Ballard, need to find a wholly original whisky for their international distribution division by visiting a number of small distillers.

A blind curve, a dangling sign, and weed-choked driveway draw Bryce directly into a truly unique opportunity. She discovers a struggling family, a shuttered distillery, and a spitfire of a daughter called home to care for her confused father.

Fiona McDougall—the only child and heir to the MacDougall & Son legacy, had her career teaching in Edinburgh curtailed by fate…or serendipity.

When the stars finally align, the two women work together to resurrect a dream for themselves and the family business—if they can weather the storms of unscrupulous business practices in the competitive whisky market.

McCall - ISBN - 978-1-948232-32-6

Sara Brighton is a quickly rising culinary star in Savannah after Food & Wine magazine named her restaurant Best New Restaurant of the South, until it burns to the ground in an accident and she impulsively packs her truck and heads for McCall, Idaho, the last place she remembers being truly happy.

Sam Draper, head of the Lake Patrol division of the McCall PD, knows the last thing she needs is another entitled tourist making her life difficult on the water. However, after Sara surprises her by helping her avoid a near professional disaster, Sam teaches her to drive a boat. The chemistry between them is hot and instant, and as the summer heats up, Sam finds herself fall-ing in love until Sara buys her late father's iconic diner and turns it into the newest hotspot for pretentious culinary tourists.

Can the love Sam and Sara found on the water survive the lingering ghosts waiting for them back on dry land?

Made in the
USA
Middletown, DE